WHERE ~~IS YOUR~~ GALLERY NOW?

Lee Benson

for Tina

Thank you

Lee

'2019'

APS PUBLICATIONS

Where's Your Art Gallery Now?
Copyright ©2018 APS Publications

Cover photograph by Egorr

APS Publications,
4 Oakleigh Road,
Stourbridge,
West Midlands,
DY8 2JX

www.andrewsparke.com

This book is dedicated to all my friends' mothers, who decided to have a big party upstairs and especially to my mom, Esta, who originally wanted six girls and a boy; I came first and scuppered her plans.

Thanks Mom, I owe you eternally

THE CANVAS

Welcome back to the gallery. We've been trading for a few years in the art world now. The gallery has bedded in and the owner has embraced a lifestyle in which stress, fun, wine and women feature heavily.

If you've already read So You Want To Own An Art Gallery, you'll need no introduction to Belinda's Aunt Charlie, who has an agenda or to a business which swims in crateloads of good wine There are new customers to meet, as well as old friends and odd nutcases, and plenty of events, including Bruce's long-planned naked exhibition. Victor is mentoring the gallery owner, my good self, in the grammar of painting and in return everyone's liable to end up tipsy on seriously good cocktails.

Maybe the latest events will want to make you consider retiring early to take up painting or fishing or whatever else floats your boat.

I will apologise if you really thought I was giving you a manual on actually how to run an art gallery because I'm afraid you'll be disappointed. What I want you to do is to put your feet up and watch me trying to make a living out of selling art.

SWAMP GREEN

'Good morning Charlie' I say with a smile.

Charlie, my able assistant Belinda's long-legged aunt, is always a good start to any morning. She's going to be standing in for Belinda for the next two weeks. Belinda's decided to take herself off for a fortnight in Sharm-el-Sheik at short notice. 'It's a bargain and I need a break in the sun.'

Two weeks with Chanel Number 5 - this will be testing.

Charlie's skirt is usually a touch too short and revealing but she does have a great pair of legs, if it's acceptable to comment on them. She also has the ability to bend over like Betty Boop in those cartoons. Her back settles at ninety degrees to her legs, which remain perfectly straight, making her hemline even shorter. Now this isn't fair at only ten thirty in the morning.

The telephone rings. I answer it. That's the division of labour round here.

'Hello is Charlie there? I must speak to her!'

'One minute.' I hand the phone over to my new assistant.

'Hello gorgeous. How are you this morning?'

This is a selling technique new to me.

After several giggles and sweet nothings - I'm not earwigging but she does fill the gallery with her voice - she politely stretches over me to replace the phone in its cradle. She stares up at the ceiling and utters an explanation of sorts; 'A woman has needs you know.'

'I'm sure we all do, but we're open for business and I don't believe that was business. Please refrain from personal calls during opening hours. Thank you.'

'Shall I make you a coffee, sour puss?'

I'm not sure this is going to be a good idea after all.

A well-dressed couple with an unruly child hollering in the pram and trying to get out of its restraints, are the first customers of the morning.

'Quiet now, Teddy. Mommy and Daddy want to look at the nice paintings.'

The child wriggles and kicks and ensures everyone knows he objects to being where he doesn't want to be.

A few quiet words in his ear might help. I put down my cup of coffee and stroll over to introduce myself.

'May I have a little word with your son?'

Go ahead' says his father, looking exhausted already.

I bend down, enjoying the spectacle of little Harry Houdini failing to release his straps, his back arching as he grunts and kicks.

'Well now,' I say in a low whisper near his ear. 'I'm Shrek's older brother and I'll put you in the swamp right under the frogs and worms and eat you up later, when you're all soaked and mouldy, with my marmite soldiers for tea.'

He freezes and shuts right up.

I stand up, turn around and smile. Grown up, 1. Child, 0.

'That wasn't so difficult. May we offer you a tea or coffee. Something stronger perhaps and would your son like a biscuit. We've got some nice ones in the kitchen?'

'A large whisky wouldn't go amiss,' the father sighs.

'Sorry, no can do. The Sunday staff drank the lot. We've got a nice drop of Rioja. It's rather smooth and somewhere in the world it's past six o clock.'

'Perfect,' says the husband.

'We'd like something a little fresh for the bedroom,' says the wife. 'Don't we darling?'

The husband looks at me with helpless eyes, irresolute in what the future holds for him. Perhaps we could organise a kidnapping of his son for a bit of peace and quiet. 'How did you do that?' he begs, desperate for the answer.

'I've had to deal with many kids in the gallery. You just say something nice to them and they're fine. It never fails.'

Meanwhile Charlie is engaged in conversation with the wife. 'What do you want in your bedroom? Oops... I mean what effect would you like to achieve?'

Yes, we aim to please anything from bordello to nun's cell.

'Over the bed or over the dressing table?'

Charlie has a unique way with phrasing. I'm unprepared for what comes next.

'I love mirrors on the ceiling and long mirrors in my boudoir. Don't you?'

The husband stares at me in disbelief. I think he's lost in wishful thinking, until the wife takes the whole situation in hand. 'We want something a little more soft and cuddly. Have you any teddy bear paintings?'

'No. I'm afraid we don't have any wildlife paintings or teddy bear picnic scenes. Would you like to take a look in my stock-room? I can show you examples of what we do have. Let Charlie look after your husband and son for a bit.'

Revenge is sweet. A few moments with a nice sane woman sans child will sooth the nerves.

'Thank you,' she says. 'That's fine, isn't it dear?'

The husband says nothing, just stares at Charlie and nods.

We walked through the back door of the gallery into the stock room.

'Wow! Haven't you a got a lot of art?'

'We believe in having a good selection to tempt those who don't see what they like on the gallery walls. Take this painting for instance.' I pull out a pastel sunset over sea.

'That's beautiful' she says. 'How did you know I'd like this?'

'It's my inner teddy bear instincts,' I smile. 'Shall we show it to your husband?'

'Yes please. And I like the look of this painting.' She points out an abstract landscape in reds and blues with purple and orange highlights.

Nothing like a teddy bear picture whatsoever!

'Right. You hold onto this one and I'll fetch that one down. Follow me!'

We return to a gallery filled with rapturous laughter and a husband practically choking at the same time.

The child still isn't making a sound.

'Sorry to interrupt the entertainment,' says the wife.

Time for me to defuse an incipient atmosphere. 'By the way, what's your name?'

'Stella. My husband is George and this is little Teddy.'

Charlie relieves the wife of the picture she's carrying. 'Can I hang it over here?' she purrs. 'I think the light would complement it. Their bedroom has a large window with soft pink curtains. Hasn't it Stella?'

'Yes, it does.' Her disapproving tone is clear to all. She glowers at her husband as if Charlie has been discovered actually in her private sanctum.

Acting to calm the incipient storm, I try to explain a little about the painters and what they were striving to achieve.

The prickly static calms and Stella expresses partiality for the pastel. 'I like this one a lot.'

'Well, that's a good start,' I say.

'How much is it?' enquires George.

'Believe it or not, it's only £850 framed in the gold leaf moulding.'

'We'll take it', says Stella, not even consulting the husband. 'Do you deliver?'

'We do. With pleasure. Where do you live?'

'Not far from Evesham,' says George.

'I live near there,' pipes up Charlie. 'I could take it to you after work.'

I think not.

I ignore Charlie's offer. 'Would Wednesday morning suit you? I'll hang it for you. All part of the service.'

'That would be much appreciated,' says Stella. George looks a tad disappointed. I bet he is.

'Wednesday it is and thank you.'

As the three of them leave, Teddy starts firing up on all cylinders again.

'Charlie, if you ever flirt with married customers again in front of their spouses, I'll ask you to leave immediately.' That's not the threat I'd far rather carry out, involving the palm of my hand and her derriere.

Charlie saunters over to me. 'Who's a grumpy teddy bear then?'

This isn't going to be an easy fortnight.

She continues, 'Why don't we go for a drink after work? Just a bottle of pink bubbles; my round. After all, a woman has needs you know.'

BURNT UMBER

A eureka moment crosses my mind. It might be a good idea to spread out. I don't mean putting on weight, that's far too easy. All you have to do is keep on drinking and enjoying life in what little time's left in an eight-day week to while away in relaxation. Oh, hang on. You think a gallery life is just sauntering in at a sociable hour of the morning, having coffee followed by a two-hour lunch break, afternoon tea and a quick snifter before strolling home for a midnight snack. Really? Tut tut! How could you!

I've received an email. Yes, we're entering the modern world. It's an invite to exhibit at a new art fair over the border in Scotland. Now the very idea of exhibiting before had petrified me, I don't know why; couldn't really put my finger on it. I suppose I always thought there were enough potential buyers to sustain my humble establishment. Still there could always be more if I take my artists to a new country with new customers. How hard can it be? The gallery's been trading for over five years now and the time seems right.

Belinda won't like it; having to take over and play at being in charge. She prefers being a support or team player as she reminds me. Often! Charlie? Well the least said about her the better. She'll just be her usual loud self, always on the lookout for a victim. For victim read customer. Anyway, they'll have to sort out the gallery without me. I'm paying them and it's only for a mere six days. Make up my mind. It's time to call a staff meeting.

Belinda is looking tanned and refreshed after her glorious sunshine holiday in the home to a million flies whilst Charlie? She's is still looking desperate.

'Ladies. I have decided to try out an art exhibition in foreign climes. Scotland to be precise.'

There's no response. Nothing. Belinda stares at me with a *you really aren't being serious sort of way* eyebrow raised in disbelief.

'Oh, how wonderful. What shall I wear?' pipes up Charlie.

I ignore her. God help me! Can you imagine working away with this woman? 'We need to select six artists and two sculptors, a few not too delicate glass pieces and a good corkscrew.'

It's a guessing game, like going up the Amazon for the first time into unexplored territory and trying to barter with semi-clad natives whilst avoiding river fever. Ok, my imagination's running a bit over-board here; it is Edinburgh, so there might not be any mosquitos.

Bit of a happy coincidence occurs. I've been doing a bit of national newspaper advertising and a chap phones up wanting to buy the painting used in the ad. And where does he live? Edinburgh, no less. Fortuitous indeed. I offer to deliver it and hang it for him. It's a good sign methinks.

Back to the list. I need a van, plenty of wine, display stands, plinths, glasses to drink from, artwork, pens, visitor book, order book and, living hopefully, the famous red dots. Add a few smart clothes, hanging equipment, a cordless drill and yes, of course, the obligatory corkscrew.

Seems quite simple, you might think.

Actually, it's considerably more difficult and requires a lot of toing and froing combined with lots of list updating and crossing offs, calls, collecting art, reassuring artists, reassuring myself (not so easy) and, you guessed it, a shed load of money up front to pay for the stand. That's the gamble. Will it work? Will total strangers buy? Will anything sell? There's only one way to find out and that's without taking Charlie along, even though the fact is, I do need someone to help out. With an assistant, maybe I could even sneak out and sketch somewhere. I doubt it but you never know. I make a few calls to some potentials and luckily, a friend I haven't seen for a while happens to be free and decides to accompany me. Oh Good! I don't have to drive.

I won't bore you with all the details. Suffice to say that we wrap everything that's required, check and check again that everything needful is in the vehicular conveyance, including me, and off we go.

It's a long way in a van that doesn't have seats that slide back. At 60 mph max, the journey's a tad tedious and we stop off at several service stations for coffee breaks.

Eventually we arrive at a magnificent old hall with vans littered everywhere. We park and survey the set up. The first person we meet is an incredibly tall woman in a tight t-shirt with the slogan *So many men so little time* emblazoned across her cleavage. 'A good start' observes Harry with a smile.

She opens her mouth and a rash of expletives pour out. Basically, the stand company have screwed up and are running behind schedule by a full day This means nothing will be ready till tomorrow and seeing as the show was supposed to open at six, there is now plenty of time to panic.

In a moment of gentlemanly consideration, we offer to buy her a drink from the bar, the one thing luckily which is open. She agrees and consumes a pint of heavy in seconds followed by another, and all before we drink more than half of our own pints. Harry is intrigued with this display of Celtic wonder, or maybe he has a fixation on large-breasted, beer-drinking women.

Suddenly, he pipes up, which is most appropriate for Scotland. You see what I did there? 'Well, if all the gallery owners get together and help out, we'll have the place ready in time.'

You know what? That's exactly what we do. Nobody knows anyone to start with, but by the end of the evening and assisted by a plenitude (that means lots) of free drinks, we paint the stands and even help the one solitary electrician available to sort out where the lights are going to be located.

Alas no time left to get any pictures displayed and everyone has to leave their wrapped stuff by their stands for the morrow. There's only one thing left to do, find our accommodation and hit the town.

The place we're staying at is a typical Georgian building, massive front door and high ceilings. A young couple who'd been gainfully employed in the banking sector, and, judging by the toys everywhere, are now into child manufacture, own the place. There are three little ones crying at different decibel levels from all over the house. Memo to self, next time look for a child-free zone to stay in. Should there be a next time.

The nanny is French and looks helplessly incapable of looking after kids. The mother, a Londoner, Mrs. Okay-Yah is not faring much better although trying her best to be so *Okay, yah* in front of us.

'Hello. Welcome to the mad house. We have three gallery owners staying with us. You've got the third floor and the others are above you. Breakfast is at eight and my husband will cook his famous porridge.' I haven't heard of it and neither has Harry so it can't be that famous. We lug our cases up the stairs, dump everything and walk out in to the cold fresh air in search of food. And a drink.

We meander through a couple of streets and come across a tavern that looks inviting. There's live music and what's more, an available table. It's very sociable and almost completely full of young and not so young people, mingling and laughing their socks off.

A well-dressed, youngish and pretty staff person greets us. 'Very good evening gentlemen. You're not from round here I see. Welcome to Margaret's. Let's get you a table and something to eat. Follow me!' She turns, flicking her ponytail aside, and leads us to the one and only empty table which is near the stage.

Harry looks around. I swear he's drooling. 'All the women here are stunning. I reckon we're in for a great few days. How many tens do you think we'll see?'

'I'm sorry. Tens? What are tens?'

'You know. Perfect tens. Stunners, crackers; great legs and all.'

A guitarist wearing jeans and a black t-shirt walks on stage and introduces himself in fluent Glaswegian. In other words, we've no idea what he's saying. However, strumming his guitar and singing in a gravelly, bluesy voice, he's well and truly impressive.

'Steak for me' says Harry 'and how about a good red?'

We've started in style, so red it will be.

Two bottles later, and two men leave in a far more relaxed mood, heading back to the guesthouse to call it a night. I open the front door and enter the hallway; the place is now blissfully quiet even if there are still plenty of toys littering the floor.

'Tomorrow at eight. Cheers, Harry' I say, climbing the stairs to bed.

It doesn't take long to fall asleep in the head-to-toe burnt umber décor. Furniture, carpet, curtains and the bed sheets! Very imaginative, I think not. My mind cries out for colour. Good job I'm wearing red socks so I drop them on to the floor so they'll be directly in my eye-line when I wake up. That turns out to be rather sooner than anticipated. I stir to a gentle knock on the door and a slight creak as it opens.

To my surprise, the au pair's standing there, dressed in a Victorian-style, white cotton nightdress. Her hair is untied and cascades down her back. She creeps over to the bed. 'Monsieur, you must excuse me. I don't know how to say zis but I am missing my boyfriend. You remind me zo much of him. I ache for him here.' She grabs her breast, sighs and without so much as a by-your leave, climbs into my bed and snuggles up rather tightly to me.

I might be dreaming of course but as I put my arm around her shoulder and feel her warm body, I realise I'm not. Neither is she an optional extra off the tariff list, such as a guided tour of ghostly old Edinburgh town.

So, what is a man supposed to do?

Well I'll put you unashamedly straight on the matter. She falls fast asleep curled up in my bed. Absolutely out cold. I trust her boyfriend doesn't have the same effect on her.

At six o clock the light pours through a chink in the brown curtains. It wakes me up. I'm alone. There is no female in the bed. *Did that really happen*. But I can smell perfume on the pillow. *Oh well*. I get up, shower, dress and walk downstairs. A brisk walk round the block seems a good idea.

'Bonjour' the au pair waves, smiling. Someone's feeling happier this morning. I never realized it was that easy to please a woman.

The sun is bright for the time of day and the trees are rustling in the breeze. It's always good to collect one's thoughts whilst walking around a city, watching it wake up. Traffic is minimal and people by and large are relaxed. In a bit all there is to do is make my stand look great, hang and display everything and prepare for the unexpected. Famous porridge time beckons. I'm feeling refreshed, if a little concerned about the strange au pair but hey, who knows what today will bring.

Porridge is served. 'Would you like whisky on it?'

'Are you serious?'

'Oh yes. a wee dram with honey sets you up for the day, trust me'.

'Ok.' Here goes.'

'Morning, Harry' A tweeded, polka-dot cravatted, blue-shirted assistant enters the breakfast room in his best suede Hush Puppies. They would be blue suede, his shoes. naturally.

Harry chirps 'I had a great sleep. Lovely big bed. You could party in it.'

The au pair walks by smiling again. *Why is she smiling?*

Mrs Okay-Yah heaves in to view so she gets my sales pitch. 'Would anyone like complimentary tickets for tonight's private view, do you think?'

'We will certainly hand out a few for you' she says.

'Is it possible to have one? I do like zeeing art?' It's the au pair.' I am a free night tonight.'

'Settled then. Here you go. See you later.'

We head for the van. I decide not to say a word to Harry about you-know-what. Just in case. Next stop; deliver the painting to the Edinburgh client.

His home isn't difficult to find. He's on Gardner's Crescent. It's a beautiful, four-story, terraced property. You can see massive chandeliers as you peer through the tall windows.

The owner opens the door in his tracksuit.

'Good morning. Special delivery.'

I offer my hand but he ignores it. With good reason. 'Sorry, I'm all sweaty. Just back from a run. Ah, come in.'

Wow what a pad. The house is exquisitely designed. He's kept all the original style and features and filled it with expensive designer furniture and fittings plus some superb antiques and modern pieces.

'Where would you like this to hang?'

'Follow me' says Paul.

We walk upstairs, along a corridor and into an empty room, freshly painted and with nothing on the walls. It brings out my inner salesman. 'Fantastic place you have here. Would you like to come along to this evening's private view? You never know, we might have a thing or two to suit. There's one fantastic piece that would look great on this wall.'

'That depends on what my wife's doing this evening' Paul says. 'She runs the diary.'

After a quick coffee and a thank you for delivering the painting followed by a smart handshake this time, we're on our way again.

'Blimey O'Reilly, what a place' chirps Harry indicating to get us out into the traffic.

The exhibition venue awash with cars, predominantly Volvos and white vans. Everyone's running around carrying artwork in bags and bubble wrap. There is loads of it. How everyone will be ready for opening time will require a concerted miracle and superhuman effort.

Suffice it to say, we manage to set up our stand within two hours, which astounds and impresses me, particularly, as opposite us are two Scottish lasses in tight jeans and t-shirts. It's a pleasure to watch them work although all they've hung are three paintings and one isn't straight. What they are is a pleasant distraction. Harry says, 'To the rescue' and armed with his cordless drill, cocked and fully charged, arranges and hangs another eight paintings for them inside approximately fifteen minutes. They're delighted, as well as being a delight to look at. Harry's obviously pleased with himself too.

Time to prepare for the show; a quick change of outfit in the gents' loo and reappearing in a slightly unconventional jacket, a loud, colourful shirt, the obligatory cufflinks and a pair of dark, almost tartan trousers - blue with green and yellow fine lines. Actually, they're golfing trousers, but don't tell anyone.

Off to the bar, which seems like a good place to start.

It's shut. Oh well there will be enough wine afterwards.

The in-house speaker system springs to life. 'Ladies and Gentlemen, the show starts in ten minutes. The organisers would like to wish all exhibitors good luck and we hope you sell plenty.'

Me too. Am I nervous or what? It feels like my gallery opening night all over again minus Miss Top Hat and Tails. Looks like shades of tartan will have to do.

Harry is chatting to the taller of the two Scottish lasses, Shona. Her assistant is Iona and they are the luck of the Celts incarnate. I've never seen tartan waistcoats look so fetching. They fit just right matched with short pleated tartan skirts. All we need now are a few single malts and we'll be St. Andrew'd out.

The doors open and a stream of private viewers flow in a direct line to the free wine. Bless the human race. They're so predictable.

In no time at all the place is packed. There are well dressed folk in tweed, well-dressed folk not in tweed, art students in an array of clothes better thrown away and one old man, well into his nineties, looks like he's walked straight out of a Spike Milligan novel, complete with hairy knees, a long kilt and carrying the knobbliest walking stick ever. His hair is silver and worn tied back in a ponytail. He's wearing massive, aged-leather boots and off-cream woollen socks. A genuine highlander, I can't understand a word he says but by any other measure he seems a nice chap.

I'm freaking though; will anything acquire a red dot tonight?

'Excuse me?' I'm suddenly brought back down to earth by a middle-aged lady in a full-length cashmere coat tapping my arm "Would you mind selling me this lovely piece of glass?'

'Not at all madam.' I let Harry write up the details as I place the first red sticker on a price label. *One down. What a lovely lady.*

And it goes on with the art we've shipped north receiving positive responses.

'Not seen stuff like this.'

'You're different. Fancy a drink after the show.'

'What's your best price on this?'

It's music to my ears. Then I spy Paul talking to the gallery owner a couple of stands down from mine. He shakes hands and is walking towards us and thankfully his wife is with him. 'Good evening' she says in a glorious accent. 'We love the painting you brought up for us.'

'I'm delighted. And your home is exquisite' I offer them a glass of my own wine instead of the venue plonk.

'Darlink' she turns to Paul. 'I think we should have these two paintings for the hall and this table too. That big one will look good in the new snug and I'm sure we could find a place for this bronze.'

Am I really hearing this? I try to remain very calm on the outside, while my insides are going Vesuvian.

Paul says 'Well ole' chap, looks like your delivery service paid off. Sort me out the price for the lot and can you deliver them tomorrow morning?'

'With pleasure. We'll be with you for nine-thirty on the nose. Is that okay?'

'Perfect. We'll have the coffee on'. He shakes my hand again and she gives me brushing kisses on each cheek. Then they leave. For a moment I'm unable to breathe. They have just agreed to buy approximately goods to half the value of the entire stand.

Meanwhile Harry has just sold another piece of glass and is looking very pleased with himself. 'That's another grand in the pot. Yes!!'

'Well done, Harry. Great sale.'

'Are you okay? You look shocked.'

I say nothing and place red dots on the sold items.

'What are you doing? You don't need to pretend we're doing even better.'

'I've just sold this lot to Paul.'

'You've got to be bloody joking.'

'No, I'm bloody well not! I'm delighted. And the good news is we have to deliver it all in the morning.'

It doesn't take long for the news of our success to travel round the show. Gallery owners and onlookers are coming by the stand to congratulate us.

'Well done.'

'Bloody 'ell, fancy that.'

'Jammy bleeders! How much did you make?'

We don't have time to rest on our laurels. The opening night may already be a roaring success but it's not over yet and there are plenty of tens about too, so we're both pleased. Nay, ecstatic.

The au pair arrives in due course. 'Allo monsieur. It is a tres belle event. Some of ze art is, how you say, eclectic. I am sinking zat I might be missing my boyfriend a lot tonight'. She winks at me. I swear, she winks before wandering off in to the now thinning crowds. The wine's all been consumed and at last the evening's private view is nearly over.

'Ladies and gentlemen the show has now closed. We look forward to seeing you again tomorrow from eleven o'clock. Please make your way to the main exit, thank you'

I pour us out two very large glasses of red. 'Thank you, Harry. What an effin' amazing evening.'

'Cheers! Did you see that woman in the black leather trousers? She gets eleven out of ten,' says Harry.

We virtually dismantle the stand, wrapping the pieces we need to deliver in the morning and then load the van before joining the rest of the exhibitors for a get together over a wee snifter.

Harry makes a beeline for the tartan sisters and I thank the organisers for a great opening event. I mean we had a great opening even if others didn't fare so well. The luck of the draw.

Harry doesn't actually succeed in pulling either of the tartan clad lassies but he's not one to give in. We return to our accommodation, unload the art into the hallway for safety and retire for the evening. 'Let's see if we can beat the figures tomorrow.' says Harry, ever the optimist.

At about one in the morning, the door opens and the au pair slips under the sheets and to let you into a little secret, Jean Pierre wouldn't approve.

The rest of the show goes almost as well as the opening session. It seems to travel by in a blur of conversation and wine, with the occasional scrap of food thrown in for good measure to ensure my able assistant keeps his strength up for whichever of the tartan-clad girls he eventually pulls. I'm not at liberty to tell you which. A gentlemen's handshake on confidentiality is his bond and what happens in Edinburgh, stays in Edinburgh.

PURPLE

Purple is a great colour, made by blending blues with reds. Conveniently, it works superbly when it comes to highlighting dangly bits. Stick with me here.

Bruce's first show is a major success. We end up selling nearly three quarters of the exhibition and he's beside himself. A new audience buy into his art and lifestyle and enable him to pay off his debts...and buy more wine.

His devotees may come from all over the world, but the buyers were mainly from my mailing list. So why am I stressed? I'm mentally and physically exhausted. It's because it's akin to running a weeklong wedding albeit without a happy couple or any in-laws. That's an unfair comparison really but we're all happy after they've all gone. And none more than yours truly.

We went through more superb wine than the restaurant next door, the only discontent being expressed by a German lady with a distinct dislike of the French. 'Why haff you no Gutt German wines here in this establishment?'

'Madam, we're an art gallery not a wine bar.' You'd never know it from all the empties by the bins.

The woman's fingers are bedecked in rings with massive stones. She's wearing a full-length fur coat, horrendously strong perfume and an overly dyed, blonde hairdo. Only the bees in the countryside would ever be impressed by her hive. She was a rather well-built woman who preferred younger men. Need I say more? For some reason she spends too much time in my gallery.

Belinda finds her a hoot. Apparently, I'm not young enough for her. I've been saved at last.

Now I have to fulfil my promise to Bruce to host his more risqué exhibition.

Okay, let me explain. What Bruce has done is to take a male wine merchant of his close acquaintance, pose him on a collection of scatter cushions, throw the odd painting into the background and paint him over and over again. Fundamentally that's the show. Ah yes, not forgetting one little detail. Said male subject is naked. That should go down well.

Whilst I'm conjuring up a plan for making it happen, a couple of well-dressed gents walk in to the gallery. They apparently been advised to check me out. Let me state at this point, the t-shirt I'm wearing features a fairly blatantly heterosexual image and even though I've no problem at all with what anybody else chooses to do in their sex lives, I have no intention of batting for the other side. I'll leave that to some of my artists, clients, and friends.

One of the gentlemen looks uncannily like the late Freddie Mercury of Queen. The other, more seriously spoken asks to see the proprietor.

'Good afternoon. I'm the owner. How may I help you?'

'My name is Derek. We're looking for something a little different. Loud but not garish!' I smile.

'I want it big and colourful. You know modern like' says the other one. We'll call him Freddie Mark II. 'We've changed our whole house round to go contemporary. Out with his glitz and glitter and in with big and bold. '

I move out of sales mode. Well actually, I start the selling process. 'I think this calls for a glass of wine. Red or white?'

'Chablis darling?' says Freddie Mark II.

Belinda doesn't wait for any instruction from me. She beats a hasty retreat via the back door, returning a few minutes later with chilled Chablis. Bless that girl; I ought to give her a raise.

'So, what have you got that's big, umm?' says Derek. *Oh no, here we go! Its double entendre day.*

'Seriously, I say 'How big would you like it? '

The banter continues and the wine does flow. Eventually after twenty minutes I offer to bring out some pieces from the stockroom. I decide to show them work by three different artists, large, colourful canvases that don't require frames. One, by a female artist, is squiggles and blobs, very tasteful, a bit like the artist. The second is a dramatic piece by Bruce and the third a really red-styled sunset with showers of golden rain cascading down one side.

Neither customer likes the last one. 'It's too loud for my taste; looks like someone's peeing up the wall.' They do like the other two. 'How much?' asks Freddy Mark II.

Now here is where you have to be tactful in guessing what the budget will be. You could ask how much someone would like to spend but it's a blatantly crude approach and besides, nobody ever wants to say how much he or she is truly prepared to spend; it could be more than they say or considerably less if they're embarrassed or showing off. I decide my approach to price should be *reasonable*. Giving a little background about the artist whilst placing the painting on the wall for viewing from another angle always looks so much more professional than the hard sell anyway.

Just then two slightly drunk and obviously camp men mince into the gallery, walk straight up to the two chaps I'm working hard on selling to and exchange kisses. 'Hello luvs; we were wondering where you'd gone.' Oh my god! A committee of buyers is never a good idea, especially when one or more is already, to put it mildly, approaching paralytic.

Little drunk man pipes up. 'How much you spending now you tart?' He turns his attention to Belinda 'Where's my drink Girl? Get me a glass of wine.'

She glares at him with the eye of an eagle about to pounce on its prey and then chooses to ignore him, heading for the kitchen in a move straight out of a movie scene. *Drop dead pal.*

'Do excuse Brenda. He's such an alkie.'

'Well' says the man now identified as Brenda. 'No booze, no stay.' He exits stage right by the main doors.

'Just a normal day in a gallery,' I say with a smile, trying to lighten up the mood.

Luckily there's no need as Freddy Mark II comes to the rescue. 'Go and catch her up and make sure she doesn't fall in the street again. Go on. We'll see you later.' The silent one obediently does as he's told. 'Now, where are we? Oh, come on; let's have them both.'

'Invoice the club and we'll pay you tomorrow' says Derek.

'A club! What sort of club?' I ask.

'Well it's not exactly a gentleman's club. Is it luv? You could come down and join us later; we always have some entertainment on a Tuesday. Everyone dresses up and has a ball.'

'Well you never know' I say sheepishly, making a shrewd guess at what sort of club it might be. Then a brilliant idea flickers through my mind. 'You don't fancy sponsoring an art exhibition, do you?'

'We'll think about it darling. I'm sure I've just spent a fortune today. Give me a day to get my lips around the idea, I'll just finish another Chablis whilst I mull. Okay?'

With such perfect timing, Belinda arrives with more chilled wine. The hauteur mobilised for *the little shit* has vanished and we're all smiles again.

As they both leave slightly the merrier, Belinda pipes up, 'I heard what you said about the club. I'll come along tonight for a laugh as long as I can come in late tomorrow.'

'For a laugh at coming in late or what?' I smile.

She takes that to mean approval. 'Okay.'

The day is done and I take a corporate decision. 'Let's have a drink.' Somewhere in the world, the sun is over the yardarm.

'I think this show will be good fun after all' That's uncharacteristically positive for Belinda. I've got a good feeling all over.

'Red, white or bubbles?' I ask.

The next day from opening to around oneish is remarkably busy probably because I'm on my own. Customers, a delivery turning up unexpectedly and the phone keeps ringing. All good if you have a team working for you, but yours truly is trying to formulate the next exhibition and I keep coming to the same conclusion. Panic. *What am I letting myself in for?*

The phone rings again, seemingly louder than the earlier calls. I answer it in my usual calm, self-assured way. Should have been a bloody actor.

'Hello. Gallery here, how may I help you?'

'Hello darling!' It's Mr No name. Freddie Mark II. 'What a night we had. You should have been there. Your little assistant was a right diva, dancing and singing on the stage, flirting with anyone and everyone. She was more or less legless when we closed up. We put her in a taxi though.'

'Really!' is all I say.

'Anyway luvy, we've decided that a big gathering at yours and an after-show party at ours would the perfect notion. Little Belinda told us what's what. We'll cover the catalogue and fizz and you can do the rest. We'd like one of the pictures to go on the bottles of bubbly. Okay! Got to go, the cat's ripping the couch again. Nothing like a mad pussy is there?' Click.

Well what do you know? The show will go on cabaret style, no less. Time to ring Bruce. No answer. He's busy, so I leave a simple message leaving out the details. Sure he'll ring back sometime within the day. When he does, it takes a lot to explain what's occurred in the last twenty-four hours but I say nothing about Belinda who walks in rather the worse for wear. In sunglasses and a veil of silence, she heads straight for the kitchen.

Bruce suggests our new sponsors should come over to the chateau to discuss it and to show them the work. I say they've already agreed and maybe it would be nicer to offer that after the show. A safer bet in my opinion. The deal is struck; we'll wait till after the exhibition and parties!

Dear Lord, forgive me; I run a simple and humble art gallery that sells art, and the like.

Of course, everyday life has to go on as well and those boring things that makes businesses run, like bills, have to be handled. There's no such thing as being allowed a day off, you know. All hail the taxman and VAT and rent and stuff. My only rant...bloody paperwork. I hate it; every bloody sheet. It would be nicer using the time to draw or paint on sheets of paper, rather than covering them in numbers.

Sorry about that. Where was I? Ah yes, nudity; always a nice topic. Subtle covering up with a touch of risqué exposure isn't too bad either. I once happened to notice a rather elegant lady walking past in a long pleated, camel skirt and white blouse, her blonde hair blowing in the wind; and the same wind caught the split in her skirt, exposing just a hint of stocking top. I nearly knocked over a statue that somehow moved right into my path. That's both subtle and risqué.

Belinda speaks. Well not exactly true. She groans. 'Oh my God!'

'Care to improve on that?' I say.

'I didn't think I was going to make it.'

'Are you referring to last night or coming in today?' I raise an eyebrow, straight from the Roger Moore manual of emotional expressions.

'Someone spiked my drinks. I mean, phew, shit, I'm still ratted but I'm here. My head! You did say I could come in late!'

'Tell me later. Get some more water down you and go and sit out the back.'

'No, sfine,' she slurs, 'I'll be okay...honest.'

This, my friend is where you take control of your staff.

I ring the chemist across the road. 'Hi Jean. Would you do me a big favour and step over to take a look at my assistant. I think someone messed with her drinks last night. She's in a right state. Don't make it too obvious you're coming to examine her. You will? Thanks.'

She calmly walks in pretending to want a present for her friend or lover. Who knows? She's not wearing a wedding ring but she's a great chemist; great legs and, I believe, a great figure under her long white coat. 'Are you all right young lady?' That's not subtle at all.

Belinda looks vacant and unwell. She appears to be grey and purple all at once. Jean picks up the phone and dials 999. Within minutes, a paramedic arrives, takes out his kit and lays Belinda down at the back of the gallery.

He's working on her properly with machines that whir and print out something. 'I think she needs her stomach pumping.' he looks up at Jean who's holding Belinda's hand in support.

'Come on, you'll be okay. What did you drink last night?'

"Shloads of Vodka, and a couple or floor shocktails. I can handle my shrink...I'm fine.' Then she passes out.

I'm delighted to report that after a trip in an ambulance and the rest of the day off, granted by her generous employer, she's fine. So much for drinking on the job. Here's a lesson to you all, drink moderately and for God's sake don't turn up to work pissed, no matter what.

CERISE

I'm seriously hoping today will be quiet so I can sort out the dreaded paperwork. Or at least that's my plan. I make myself a fresh coffee, Java blue mountain, and sit down at my desk. Here goes; computer on, floods of emails and...a woman walks in.

'I have to show you my work...I absolutely insist. I've come all the way from Chelsea. Are you listening?'

Good grief. She hasn't even said *hello*.

I look up to be confronted by a tall, middle-aged woman dressed with attitude in thick woolly tights, pink Doc Martins, a very short woollen skirt, also pink, and a cerise scarf with her hair tied in a bun. You couldn't miss her in a crowd. Oh yes and a purple blouse with odd shaped and different coloured buttons.

That's the thing about art. It's all in the observation.

'Young man. I'm talking to you. Come here now.'

Oh no. My coffee will go cold. I was so looking forward to the caffeine rush I so desperately need.

I have to say it, just as I know what the answer will be. 'Good morning! Have you an appointment?'

'Don't be ridiculous? I want to see the art buyer or the owner, now!'

'He's not in today' I reply. She looks scary; her behaviour is scary and, I've a feeling, her art will be scary too.

'How old are you?' She eyes me up and down.

'I'm approaching a milestone birthday sometime in the next few years.' I attempt a smile but don't quite pull it off.

'Do you realise I have boys like you for breakfast?'

'That's nice. I prefer smoked salmon and scrambled eggs with a large orange juice.'

This is mad. Surely, she's not for real

'Do you have many girlfriends?'

'Do excuse me. I don't believe I can be of any assistance to you. If you'd like an appointment then I'll see when the owner is free.'

She ignores me and continues. 'What do you think of these then?' With that she undoes all the non-matching buttons of her blouse and exposes her breasts, right in front of my face.

Now I have to say they are mighty impressive and by any standard look real. Gravity isn't ruining her cleavage anyway.

'Don't you find art makes you horny...I do.' She undoes her bun, flings her head back and takes a deep breath. 'God it's good!'

I'm looking on in disbelief. *Someone help me please.* It's only Wednesday.

'You'll have to do' she sighs, unzipping the folder of the type we commonly refer to as a portfolio. 'Let me present my art.'

She's plainly not about to take no for an answer and strews sheet after sheet onto the floor. Each shows a naked torso.

'These look like they're of you,' I say.

'I love to see myself in the mirror. I have four in my studio. You should come and see me work sometime. Take a day off. I could paint you with me as well.'

Actually, despite the performance, her work isn't that bad. A bit raunchy obviously but much less dramatic than her entrance. In this context, that's a good thing.

'Madame' I say, rising from behind my desk. 'I shall tell the owner you'd like to see him and you may now put your work away, if you don't mind. Thanks.'

'I do mind.' She continues to produce more work from her bulging folder. There are couples in various coital positions and then she tops the lot with a drawing of herself naked on a horse.

No. I won't ask her if the horse was in the studio despite my inner devil cajoling me to do just that.

'Have you a CV?'

'No. But I do have a massive bed in Chelsea when you visit. Plenty of room.'

'I'll...uh...tell my boss that.' I thinking you'd need to get seriously fit to visit her studio. *Please go*, I'm screaming out in my head. On the outside I'm smiling and trying to look bored. I'm obviously failing.

'When will he be back? I can wait a while.' She really doesn't take no for an answer.

I feign a flick through the diary.' Says he'll be in on Saturday afternoon. You're welcome to wait but we tend to close up at night.'

At last she shows a sense of disappointment. I begin to think I can actually bring this episode to an end. She looks at me thoughtfully and says 'Well if you're staying, I'll stay.' *Oh, my giddy ruddy bloody aunt!!* She walks across and grabs my crotch. 'Don't play with my feelings. You know you want me. My trains at five forty-five. We have time.'

Luckily, and I mean extremely luckily, right then a rather petite lass walks in holding hands with her chap. 'Are we disturbing you?'

'Not at all please come in.' I bow. A warm sweeping welcome.

'Yes, you are!' Says the demonic life-drawer from hell.

Thankfully they're not easily deterred. 'We'll just have a look round.'

'Would you like a drink?' I offer. 'Wine or coffee?'

Before they can answer, Madame pipes up. 'You never offered me anything to drink. Or anything else for that matter.' She snorts loudly.

'Correct ...And I believe you're just leaving'

And this is what you call an ordinary day at the gallery? I pour the coffee down the sink, sod the paperwork and serve myself a large glass of wine.

BLONDE

Charlie looks like an eagle about to pounce. 'He's mine all mine.' She means the tall blonde young man who's just walked in. He's trendily dressed with a crisp white shirt and dark blue jeans that leave nothing to hide in the box department. Even the sun is shining on his immaculately quiffed hair-do

'Good morning,' she says with a tone of voice reserved in her sub-basement. 'May I help you.' He stops and eyes her up from head to tail and back again. We men are so obvious but then, as a friend of mine reminds me, Women are the way they are so men can look at them. *Comments on a postcard please!*

'I've just moved into the area and found you as I was walking around town.' Charlie's drooling. Poor chap stands not a hope in hell of escaping her clutches.

'Let me show you around the gallery and if you're at a loose end, I could show you round the area. I know all the right watering holes.'

'That would be great. We're filming for three weeks and it does get so boring afterwards.' Who's chatting up whom? He's a real smoothie. Charlie offers him a drink. On me! Naturally he accepts and they're chatting away. *Sell girl: sell!* She places her arm over his and walks him to the stock room 'I think we've the perfect thing for him' she says as she passes me, taking her victim to her lair.

Eight minutes pass and they return somewhat dishevelled with two pictures and an air of something having gone on. *Eight minutes?* Umm! I'm saying nothing.

Mike; his given name is Michael; sits down like a naughty school boy. Charlie is still fussing over him but to give her credit, she's hanging the two paintings on the wall as a potential sale. 'What do you think of these?' she preens.

He regains his composure enough to rise and walks over to view the pictures properly. 'I'm not so sure about that but I love this one.' He points as if performing on stage. 'May I collect it later?'

'Sure fire. We close at six tonight.'

'That's great. I'll buy you a drink later to celebrate.' He spins on his heels and exits central stage.

She looks at me with an air of satisfaction. 'That didn't take long did it?'

Now then. What was she talking about? Eight minutes! I shan't say a word. Honest.

Six o clock arrives and there's no sign of our actor. Charlie is looking dejected and rejected when suddenly blondie lands, a fashionable ten minutes late. 'I'm so sorry. You know how it is.'

A smile radiates all over Charlie's mush. *You know how it is. Tonight's going to be a good night.*

Time to leave her to it. 'I'm off me dears. Have fun'.

'Oh no. I insist you join us for a snifter!' says Mike.

Gallerists don't do chaperoning as a rule but why not. 'Just the one 'I reply.

We walk off to the nearest saloon

Set 'em up barman Cut.

ELECTRIC BLUE

I look up through the glass front door. It's a fairly ordinary sort of day; a bluish sky with a smattering of clouds against the background rumble of the city drifting by. And then to my surprise and pleasure, five girls walk into the gallery. Their names are Cindy, Sophie, Serena, Smiley and George. How do I know this? Well their names are emblazoned across their chests.

They speak and giggle in a sort of alternating unison. 'We're organising a charity run-walk-mash up, around the town and we want to use your gallery as a refreshment stop. All you have to do is sponsor a page and we'll include your logo on our t shirts and bring you in loads of people.'

Now there's a nice thought. Justified PR expense. Can't wait to tell the accountant the news.

'With pleasure ladies, in a good cause.'

The day arrives and two boxes of mixed cocktails in vials are delivered. They are horrendous shades; Glowing Green and Florescent Red with dashes of Electric Blue. God knows what's in them or what they'll do to you. But as the gallery motto states, put colour into your life.

We wait like a refuelling stop and wait and wait some more.

Suddenly a rosy-cheeked chap, sporting a long blonde wig, sweating profusely, in his pink leotard and black fish net stockings with the most incredibly high heels, staggers in through the doors.

'What an f-ing stupid bet eh? Drink now, please. These shoes are killing me!'

'The sight of you isn't exactly doing us any favours either,' I laugh, recognizing him as the MD of a local architects' practice. Think the last time I saw him was dressed in a kilt in a gay bar after a Burns night. Now he's at it again!

Within minutes the place is a heaving mass of fancy dress and outrageous costumes. It closely resembles a Rocky Horror reunion party. Stockings, heels tight bodices leather and satin, the lot. And that's just the chaps.

The women fare a little better. At least their legs are clean-shaven. Mind you, the odd lass has a bit of stubble but who's noticing? Or dares comment?

Smiley walks in, smiling divinely. She has a proper polished ring of white-toothed confidence. 'My logo looks great on you' I say admiring her electric blue T-shirt. Or the physique inside it.

'Do you mind if I hang around for a bit?'

'With pleasure' I say.

She looks into my eyes 'Come closer '

I'm already standing right in front of her. 'How much closer would you like?'

'Much nearer'

You couldn't put a ten-pound note between us. She pulls my head down to hers and plants a smacker of a kiss on my lips.

She doesn't let go either but continues to kiss me and mess up my hair.

'Thank you. That's my challenge fulfilled. Fancy an encore?'

'I'm not complaining.' Smiley kisses me again.

'I've got to go and catch up with the gang. Bye'

Just like that. Gone

Belinda pokes me in the ribs. 'You've just passed the snog challenge,' she says.

'I'm not complaining,' I smile

COLOURS OF SUMMER (Part 1)

A letter arrives with a printed stamp from The Houses of Parliament. I'm invited to a party at the House of Commons. I love a good party. Been known to throw the occasional one myself, sorry private viewings I mean, not parties at all, as far as the taxman's concerned. This looks like it's going to be rather different.

There's a personal note attached to the invitation. *Do you mind being our guest list bouncer/ organizer?* Well I suppose it's a great way to get to meet everyone. I immediately ring to accept and say I'll be delighted to play the role of doorman!

Two minutes later the phone rings. 'Hello ol' boy. I've been thinking. You're a passionate salesman and you know your art but you don't understand the grammar of painting so I think you should come out to our next painting school to learn it. You can throw in the odd lecture as well. What do you say?'

Good grief I think. I get to paint abroad? How Wonderful! Sunshine, the odd glass of wine, painting and relaxing, my dream come true or what?

'When?'

'It's short notice but you won't regret it. Three weeks on Thursday' Regret it? In my mind I've already packed.

'Let me see if I can get a flight. And yes please.'

'Splendid.'

'Where is it?'

'Tuscany, dear chap, where else! Would you mind bringing out marmite and some rough-cut marmalade?'

'Consider it done.'

The line goes dead, there's no goodbye. Short and to the point. Check the dates. Typical! The party in London is on the Tuesday night so I'll have to dash back Wednesday and be at the airport for 6 am Thursday. Who says gallery life is boring?

Bruce rings again, 'I've booked a flight this Saturday. Shall I bring some cheese and mustard?' Life in the fast lane eh!

Sometimes I wish my pace of life would be a bit slower but who am I kidding? It's been like this ever since opening the doors of the gallery. I'm brought back into the moment as a couple of customers stroll in. 'Greetings my dears, wonderful day isn't it. You look like you have a gap on your wall to fill?' They don't. They're just mooching to kill time and are soon gone.

Belinda, in front of the computer, confirms a flight for me and queries my return date. 'How long this time?'

'It's only for ten days.' I try to sound casual. 'You can have this whole weekend off, if you like, with pay!'

'Sweet talking sod. Okay, you're booked. You fly into Pisa.' She presses the return key and signs out. I'm off to lunch.' My generous offer means another whole weekend with Charlie. Oh dear!

Bruce arrives at precisely wine o clock, towing a small luggage bag on wheels, and sits down at the desk. We'd be having a quiet day except that Charlie seems louder than usual, Effervescent she calls it. F'ing annoying I think.

'Oh, he's nice, just my type.'

'Charlie, I hate to disappoint you...' I stop, mid-sentence. Let the fun begin. She'll learn. 'Charlie this is Bruce. Bruce say hello to Charlie' I take a corporate decision to close for lunch. 'Come on, let's get a bite to eat. You too Charlie.'

'How fabulous.'

Bruce looks at me gone out, as they say in Sheffield. I put a sign on the door saying *Gone fishing. Back later.* Sometimes you have to seize the moment.

We stroll across to a little French restaurant and dig in for the afternoon. 'Fizz all round. Let's celebrate something.' Charlie's sitting near Bruce on the bench seats. Her skirt has risen and she makes no attempt to cover her thigh. You have to give her credit; she does possess a mighty fine pair of pins. Purely a natural observation! Bruce, however, is excited about what his show entails and ignores Charlie's exposed expanse of thigh. *Wine, women, men, whatever and song.* Although on a serious note, we'll be drinking some superb wines at the event again - always a plus. The show will be different but I'm now braced for this; I've started to line up all the gods of retail and more besides. *So, help, please let this be a success.*

Charlie's still unaware of the exhibition's content. 'It's predominantly the male nude,' I say in a low voice.

'Fanbloodytastic' she says. 'Let's celebrate dangly bits. My favourite pastime.' The champagne's already gone to her head.

Bruce is almost beside himself; not amused in the slightest. 'It's all about the trust and relationship within the art.' He takes a gulp of prosecco 'Who's she anyway?'

'Charlie's my part time assistant and can be very good in her own way.' I'm not going overboard in her defence.

'Mr. Bruce. This show is about sex and sex sells. Okay. However you want to wrap it up and explain it, is fine, but sex is my specialist topic and that's that'. She raises a glass.

He smiles at last, 'She's right. Charlie you're right. Cheers.'

I think it's time to change the subject. 'I'm going to paint in Tuscany for ten days. Rather excited to say the least.'

'I doubt you'll gain much insight in ten days and as for the wine...' He's such a wine snob. 'Although I've enjoyed many a good Italian red.' Bruce is obviously thinking of himself again but quickly brings the subject back to the exhibition once more. 'When will the catalogue be ready?' That's the thing with most artists; it's all about them. There's an inbuilt rivalry. I shan't call it jealousy for fear of being shot. After all, I'm only a gallery owner and apparently in their eyes, all I should do is sell art. Just you wait. One day it will be me and my art, not anyone else's. If I ever get the time that is to have a life outside the four walls of my retail establishment?

'Well Bruce ol' boy, you can judge what I do when I return. How's that? Touché!' The waiter arrives just at the right moment for refills all round.

'Let's have a bottle of French wine,' says Bruce, just one more hint of his distaste for most things Italian in his suggestion.

The rest of the lunch meanders by, aided by several glasses and Bruce is mellowing to the presence of both a dominant woman and a gallerist who wants to be an artist. We're about to leave when, by sheer chance, Freddy Mark II and partner stroll in, see us and come over. 'Darlings, how are you?'

'Well! What great timing. Let me introduce you to Bruce.'

Everyone kisses cheeks and another bottle of champagne is suggested, agreed to constitute a sound idea and called for. A magnum arrives and we chink away the afternoon. Bruce is back in his element; the men love him to bits as he revs up his performance levels and talks about his work, his home, his life his dogs, his wine...zzzzzzzz.

Still, it's all PR and they're paying for the sponsorship so perhaps we can dispute it being time wasted.

Charlie holds her booze far too well. That is until she decides to stand and duly falls backwards into Freddie Mark II's lap. 'Love the shoes babe,' says Derek as Charlie's legs fly high in the air. Everything else was on show too but no one said a word. It's good to know there's still chivalry towards the fairer sex.

'Oops! I think I'm a little tiddly. How's that happened?' She dusts herself down and realigns her skirt but remains none too steady on her heels as she carefully heads off to powder her nose.

'She's so camp' says Derek. 'Do let her work the exhibition as well.'

A second magnum later and we're all a tad merry. I decide to put Charlie in a cab and send her home.

'I say chaps, that's both my assistants you've rendered pissed.'

'Well, you only live once' says Freddy Mark II. 'I'm so looking forward to our show.'

We get up to leave for the second time, rather more intoxicated and considerably later than planned. Who cares? We stroll back to the gallery and there's a couple browsing through the window. 'Hope you've not been waiting too long?' I say unlocking the front door with a certain measure of difficulty, trying to present a moderately sober front.

'We've been admiring that bronze over there,' the woman says, pointing to a sculpture on a plinth in the middle of the gallery. 'How much is it?'

The alcohol is working too well. 'A mere twenty-four thousand pounds, madam. With a free bottle of wine.'

'Well darling, it's what you've always wanted.'

'I know,' she says looking lovingly into his eyes, but its …'

'Shush.' He holds her hand tight and turns to me. 'We love it. If I pay now, would you mind delivering it tomorrow?'

Would I mind!!!!!!!!!! There's only one thing to say. 'It will be my absolute pleasure. What time would you like it?'

'Say tea time. We should be back by then'. He presents his credit card, which clears without question.

'I know I shouldn't but hey this calls for a celebratory drink. Champagne Okay?'

The woman glances at her chap and we all hear her quietly say 'I do love you.'

Cheers everyone. The sun is almost shining even if it hasn't reached the yard arm yet so I'm happy. Not such a bad day after all. 'Where shall we go for supper?' Bruce looks up from his book as if totally unimpressed with the latest sale.

'Jesus! Let's sober up first.'

Sunday arrives far too quickly for my liking. My brain feels a little cloudy, to say the least, but I am compos mentis to open the gallery. There's no sign of Charlie, and I vaguely remember telling Bruce not to come in before midday. At eleven-fifteen Charlie arrives in a white trouser suit wearing the obligatory dark glasses. For the first time in her life probably, she's reserved. By this I mean I get a simple quiet 'Good morning,' as she heads to the back of the gallery to make coffee. There are small mercies in certain staff being hungover. But hey, I'm not the sort of guy who'd take advantage of such an opportunity. Much. 'How's the head?' I call out. Loudly.

She comes back in and sits, all in slow motion but all she says is 'Why is he gay? What a waste of a male specimen. Oh, my head isn't talking to me! I don't seem to remember much of what happened yesterday?'

'Let's not debrief on that now. Please sort out this side of the gallery; it could do with a change around. You'll feel much better if you do something.'

'Thanks for lunch yesterday. What I remember of it.' Charlie stands and surveys the place. Well, I have to hand it to her, she's a true soldier and slowly comes back to life, regaining her ability to function, along with the gradual re-emergence of her natural loudness.

Bruce strolls in around one o'clock and stops Charlie working to show her some of the paintings. In the end I send him off to lunch on his own because we've work to do, and by a whisker at four o'clock the place looks superb.

One thing always works. As you move something around it takes on a fresh look and looks new. I don't understand galleries where the same paintings hang for months in the same place.

And to prove it works a chap saunters in and stops by one of the freshly relocated paintings. 'This wasn't here last week, was it?'

'No sir. New in. What do you think?' Always engage with the customer.

'I've been looking for something like this for ages.'

Bless him. Wrap it up Charlie. Job done.

We close up and Charlie gives me a kiss on the cheek. 'Thanks again for yesterday; you're a sweetie'.

I escort Bruce to the station and head off to deliver the sculpture from yesterday's only sale. The one that made my day.

COLOURS OF SUMMER (Part 2)

Tuesday and I'm driving to London.

I hate driving but at least I can an exit the party when I like, a quick getaway so to speak. The city has a complete different set of road rules to the rest of the country I find. I'm not one for living in the fast lane and almost enjoy the sense of bumbling around like a country yokel. The result is that I'm undertaken, overtaken and sworn at in far too many languages Anyway I eventually arrive at my destination, a reserved parking space. How cool and I'm not even a member of parliament! I'm unable to share the exact location as it's a sworn secret and only the invitees know.

For the occasion I'm wearing my loudest shirt, bought for a bet with a friend who said nobody could get away with wearing it. Wrong! I win and I certainly stand out tonight.

I'm greeted with 'Fuckin hell! Who put you up to that?' I rest my case.

The guest list is three pages long. I don't personally know many of the names but I recognize at least 88% of the invited partygoers. I'm thinking this will be fun and as if by magic a large whiskey is placed in my hand. I know, I'm driving. But I need to look the part and I don't have to really drink it.

The order of play is as follows:

1. Let them in
2. Anything goes
3. Speeches
4. Food to order; no idea what that entails
5. Party hard
6. Leave discreetly

Within minutes, there are politicians, musicians, actors and every other manner of celebrity queuing up. I recognise a famous singer who's not on the list. He's clearly on his own and as I say, he's not on the list. This is cool. 'I'm sorry' I say. 'Invitees only.'

The response is the anticipated one. 'Do you know who I am?'

I do but I dislike his band and his music. Now I know how bouncers feel. Great. 'Hang on. I'll have to check.' Get on the handset.

'Is he on his own or has he got an entourage with him'

'Solo.'

'Fuck it. Okay.'

I tell him it's alright this time. He's not impressed in the slightest but *it's my job, mate.* Good grief. How many times do you hear that expression?

One stunning lady is already half cut, wearing a very short dress, ridiculously high heels and is bouncing off other guests. She lurches over to me. 'Where have we met?'

Well I'm sure I've never sold her anything. Nor have I ever appeared on her show.

'Remind me?' I try to steady her. She titters, leans over too far and falls into my arms.

'I'm sorry; I can't remember.'

She shoves me, harder than expected, back against the wall. 'You're not supposed to forget me, that really hurts.'

'I don't believe I've had the pleasure. Maybe you're mistaking me for someone else or someone else looks like me.'

'Shame.' She staggers off.

The temptation to drink that whiskey is getting stronger, but guests are still arriving. I feel like calling out 'Next!'

One old doddery chap looks like a politician and acts like one asking for a seat. I suspect his enormous bulk could shatter one of the old chairs littered around. However, I pull one over and he plonks himself down, beads of perspiration free-flowing from his brow as he pulls a red spotted handkerchief from his jacket pocket and absorbs his instant shower. Yuck.

Next up a group of luvvies all behaving in a frivolous manner and indulging in the worst dress code you can imagine. Do I need to amplify? No, I don't and actually, apart from the fact that they're obviously gay thespians, they turn out to be hilarious.

The place is filling rapidly, and only a few names remain which aren't crossed off. Virtually a full house. It's loud, boozy, smoky and blissfully entertaining. Most people don't know who I am and that makes it an even more amusing place to be.

Our host decides to hold court, shouting out, 'All right you lot. Quiet for a moment! As you know our time has come to move out of here. It's been fun with a few tough encounters you might say.' There's a massive cheer from everyone.

'I'm retiring from office and looking forward to relaxing full time.' Huge sighs and cries of *Shame. You'll never retire.*

'You'll all have to come and visit us up north. Right who wants food; hands up for burgers.'

There's a fast food takeaway a few doors away, and within minutes an array of chips, burgers, with cheese and without, fish and pies have been ordered and to get people started, a young lass brings around a tray of smoked salmon on very small brown bread pieces. A few minutes later and she returns sing the very glass charger I presented months ago to our host, as a tray. Well you might as well. 'Please don't drop it' I whisper to the lass,' It's valuable and I can't replace it anymore.'

The place ends up smelling just like a takeaway caff, the only difference being the alcohol and tobacco fumes.

I notice a couple embracing, and that's putting it mildly, on the stairway. She's not complaining as he practices his octopusical tendencies with limited success. That's show business.

I notice the party is beginning to quieten down and people are forming groups by profession. Isn't that weird how humans stick together. A gentleman in a yellow tweed suit and blue spotted bow tie, with a waxed handlebar moustache, approaches me with two drinks in his hands, 'I've noticed you're not drinking much. Here, I've brought you a rather nice red.'

'Most kind but I've got a long drive later.'

'Well, you could always come and stay at my pad. It's not far!'

Hells teeth, all these lovely female actresses and I get hit on by a colour-blind, badly dressed, old queen.

'Do I look gay to you?' I ask.

'Don't knock it till you try it love.'

'Sorry to disappoint you but I'm full time hetero in spite of my shirt.'

'It's so you though.'

'Thank you. I wore it for a bet.'

'Well, if you want to change your mind, here's my card.' He presents it with a flourish as though expecting a fanfare or drumroll.

'And if you ever want to purchase art, I've a gallery.'

Our host puts her hand under my arm, 'Come and meet a great friend of mine.' She pulls me into the front room and there, sitting on the floor, are two musicians I certainly recognise.

'He's a painter too and was scared to talk to you. Weren't you Thomas?'

'Love your music' I blurt out.

'Thanks. I've never shown anyone my art before. It's not like performing on stage or even being on TV, like. It's sort of more personal. Do you get my drift?'

'Totally' I agree. 'I dream about showing my own work, but I sell stuff far superior to mine. You're welcome to come up and show me your work or I can always come to see what you do wherever you are, assuming you're in the UK. Or if not, you could always pay my fare,' I laugh.

'Seriously. Hey that's a done deal, man.'

Work stops for no man, party or not. In fact, there are several musicians who have studied art and some are great. I wonder what his'll be like?

I would love to be the artist, I really would. I let the thought meander around my head. Maybe one day.

I'm so sorry.' Classic English shorthand for *I'm off, I really must be leaving you all.*

'You've been a hoot', or host says and she gives me a big hug.'

I slope off and head for my reserved parking space. There's a Policeman on duty standing by my car. 'This yours, sir?'

'Yes, officer.'

'Been partying, have we?'

'You could say that.'

'Drink much?'

'Not a drop.' The bloody truth. The large whiskey is untouched where I left it. I knew the gods were looking after me.

'Think I should breathalyse you, then.'

Oh, I've waited for this moment. 'With pleasure, officer. I've not had a drink since the weekend.'

'Go on then, bugger off. Don't park in this space again. They're reserved for special personnel.'

I think about putting him straight but say only 'Good night.' Open the door, sit down, belt up, smile and drive away.'

Say no more, apart from one thing, I'm bloody starving. Bloody burger takeaways, not bloody likely. Not like our receptions for sure. I put *The Who Live At Leeds* on loud and drive home, tummy rumbling in time to Keith's drumming.

COLOURS OF SUMMER (Part 3)

The next day I'm feeling somewhat shattered. It's all catching up with me.

'Morning boss,' Belinda hisses like I've done something wrong.

Do I detect irony or something? I wait and say nothing

"I hear I missed a fab weekend. Charlie rang and told me everything.

'I'm sure that's not entirely true. She didn't even remember getting back home. It was a little OTT.'

'A little!!!!'

I felt like saying that Charlie had drank enough for the England rugby squad, first and second teams but hold back. 'Your aunt was smashed in front of Derek and Freddy Mark 2. She thought she could add Bruce to her list of conquests and without trying, failed. Hey, but did she tell you, we sold the Roderham bronze.'

Belinda wants reassurance about my pending absence. You're in charge. Tell Charlie when she's to come in. There's some cash out back for whatever and we still have plenty of wine. I'm sure you'll be brilliant and sell lots. You've got all my details - where I'm staying and I believe there's internet access there. Am I missing anything?'

'It's not a good time to tell you this, but I think I want a change of direction '

Oh, bloody hell, that's the thing when you employ people, you're never really in charge and anything can and does happen. 'Listen, you're brilliant, and I for one would not stop anyone chasing whatever they want out of life. Just one question. Will you stay till after I get back please?'

'Of course, I wouldn't drop you in it. I have to apply for this course in October, so I can stay till then. Okay?'

Nothing but nothing is going to ruin this opportunity to paint; if necessary I'd have closed up for a week. But it's still a bombshell that's reverberating Well with this bombshell in my mind as I set off to pack and get ready for an adventure. Now where is Castiglione della Pescaia again? Tuscany's a big place after all.

I have to be at the airport ridiculously early, too early for a pint of Guinness at breakfast even. The plan is to meet up at Pisa airport and then the group will travel on by mini bus. The flight's on time and blissfully nothing untoward occurs on board apart from a chatty stewardess called Moira who lives in Swords, just outside Dublin. I know this as she says it all in one breath and, by the time the plane touches down, I've had a detailed breakdown of her entire life and family plus the three dogs and a horse. I only asked for a coffee with a Jameson's.

Pisa is a mad airport. You don't know who's leaving and who's landing, and everyone mingles irrespective of destination. I aim for the nearest bar, order a real espresso and read up about where we're going. There is nothing like being prepared and you're right to think it; I'm nothing like prepared. Think non-stop gallery life is easy? Why don't you try it sometime? Want to buy mine?

We're going to a fishing port. According to the newspaper it hasn't been discovered by the British yet. *Oh good, no English bars*. The thing about Tuscany is it's renowned for good wine and food - no egg and chips and pints of lager.

I'm people watching and lose track of time. I spy an elderly, very English looking couple standing in the middle of the walkway. He's sporting straw hat, cravat and yellow trousers with an old wrinkled linen jacket. Perfect old school, late sixties to mid-seventies and she's wearing a two-piece, floral pleated dress and matching jacket and she too sports a large-brimmed, straw hat. I walk over and ask if they're part of the painting group. Of course they are. Within minutes we're talking art. They have already been informed about me and my gallery. Or should that be forewarned?

A few moments later another couple of similar age in nearly identical attire appear followed by two lovely ladies straight out of some old Women's Institute poster. They're laughing and enjoying being alive it would appear. They make me feel rather young and gauche by comparison. Next to arrive is a teacher - well she looks like a teacher, maybe a head mistress, with her dark-dyed, chestnut hair pulled back into a tight bun. She's wearing an overly long skirt in drab green, a white cotton blouse, and a tweed jacket, with that velvet collar. She's straight out of St Tinian's.

Our host, Victor arrives in much the same garb as the other men except that his cravat is red and he's escorting a rather lovely looking middle-aged lady, he introduces as Penelope. She is very smartly dressed and certainly stands out. Methinks it's a classic Chanel number.

'Right, we're all here now. Follow me' says Victor and 'Good to see you ol' chap.'

'Likewise,' I say.' The marmite is in the case with the Oxford English marmalade in case you were worried.'

'Super.'

We head to the car park and a battered and beaten-up old Ford transit. The seats have seen better days and one rear door is held on with wire. 'Don't worry about her, she's fine, never let me down yet.'

'Are you going to drive,' I ask '...or have we got a driver?'

Victor looks at me sheepishly so I volunteer to drive. 'Just as long as you tell me which way to go.'

'With pleasure. Mind third gear it bounces out occasionally.'

It doesn't take too long to acclimatise to Italian style driving even with nine other GB passengers aboard. Use the horn and put your foot down. The journey takes approximately an hour and a half with the last bit all up-hill. The art wagon makes it, and we arrive at a large, typically Tuscan villa with shuttered windows and large doors. It's been recently repainted - say no more than two decades ago - but looks inviting in what you might call a shabby chic sort of way.

I look out over the bay, a stunning vista, and there's a large patio to sit out on whilst enjoying the scenery. There's a fountain, in working order and, hidden behind tall pines, a swimming pool. *Wow* is the word that comes to mind.

Plastic goblets filled with rose wine appear carried by a little bent lady called Liliana. She speaks no English and nods all the time. Victor coughs, taps a spoon and commands our attention. 'Welcome. Firstly, it should be a lot of fun. Secondly, I hope you manage to paint some future masterpieces and thirdly please drink as much wine as you like. Do help yourself. The fridge is always full. Supper will be at seven tonight. We have two more joining us later, as they're driving up from Rome.'

We're given our bedroom keys and then chill and mingle on the patio. Emily and Libby, the two giggling sisters, are still laughing out loud, 'We haven't been to Rome in years'. This makes them giggle even more.

I'm intrigued by the first couple who are rather quiet. We haven't been properly introduced yet. 'How was my driving then?' I try to start up a conversation.

'My wife isn't a good traveller. How do you do by the way? I'm

Charles and my wife is Gladys.'

'It was a bit bouncy in the back' says Gladys.

We're so English, we never swap names at the beginning unlike the Americans, who ram their name down your throat as many times as they can in as little time as possible. I prefer our reserve.

'We own a little place in Portugal, still making port, but the children tend to run things now. She's the artist. I'm here for the sun.'

'I must confess to loving the odd bottle of port...once opened and all that.'

'This is my first painting holiday. I'm so nervous.'

I decide to venture up to my room. It's on the middle floor at the end of the landing. I open the door and the view that greets me is stunning. The windows face straight out to sea. I'm in heaven. The room is old and original. When I sit on the bed, the mattress too is old and original. I lie on it and crash out within seconds.

I sleep for two hours, waking up not knowing where I am. Ah yes, Tuscany by the sea. A quick change, freshen up and off downstairs. Everyone is dressed for dinner, except me. Oops! I'm on holiday for heaven's sake. We are all finally officially introduced to each other and move onto the patio

The table is set with tea-lights everywhere and the sun vanishes in minutes, the sky going a blue-black and the stars twinkling above. You can just hear the sea. It's truly magical. Supper is served at a leisurely pace, comprising endless glasses of wine, a Tuscan bean soup, veal and potatoes. To finish, we're offered Castagnaccio, served with a pudding wine, the classic Tuscan dessert.

Ten days of this and I shan't fit into any of my clothes.

Eventually Victor pushes his chair back, stands up from the table and says, 'Breakfast is at seven and the first talk will be at eight-fifteen on the patio. Remember to bring your notebooks. There's a night cap inside for anyone who wants one.'

We all move inside, the two giggling ladies bid good night and head for the stairs. The port couple, Charles and Gladys, follow suit and the rest of us sit around to partake in the green liquid Liliana pours from a tall shaped bottle into little glasses. She then utters something in Italian and leaves the room. Victor says she was wishing us a good time here in her home.

So, she actually owns this magnificent place and isn't the maid. I'm even more impressed.

The nightcap is rather moreish and we share a couple of top up rounds and suddenly it's one o'clock. Definitely time to retire.

Penelope is in the room next to mine. 'Isn't Victor sweet?' she says opening her door. 'Night sweetie.'

'Good night,' I reply.

Then it's six o'clock. My love of early mornings is zero and this is the second one in a row but the sun is already shining, driving shafts of light through the wooden shutters. At least I'm not the last one at the table for breakfast. If only just.

Victor's wearing red cords; check shirt and a bright orange cravat. Penelope looks stunning again, straight out of *Vogue*. I'm in T-shirt and shorts. The garb of the others falls in between our extremes.

When the classes begin, I'm seriously nervous. It's like being back in school, and I didn't enjoy school first time around. Some of the group are experienced painters; the rest of us are mere beginners but in minutes, Victor's entertaining anecdotal method of teaching relaxes us all. An hour flies by and we're told to find locations around the villa to paint whatever we like. That's it.

Where to start? The problem is that Penelope isn't far from me and provides a pleasant distraction. She's let her long hair down and is sitting cross-legged in a skimpy pair of shorts. Such a shame today is about landscape and isn't a life class.

Lunch, more talk, more wine, siesta, more painting. See my dears, it's not all work. I'm loving it.

Day three and another early start. We all head off in the van to Siena. We're going to the central piazza known as Il Campo, for lunch. It's about an hour and a half normally by car but Victor drives considerably slower than nearly every other vehicle on the planet and talks all the way about the history of the place. He does however claim to know the best restaurant to eat in and the best views to paint. We eventually arrive in Siena after Victor breaks his personal best record of two hours and disperse each to do our own artistic thing.

Whilst minding my own business, sitting on a little fold up seat and trying to look like I know what I'm doing, an old man in dungarees and an even older oil-skin jacket places himself behind me. He starts to talk in Italian tutting and commenting on every brush stroke I'm making. It's totally distracting.

'Anglesi?'

'Yes.'

'You are not so bad. Why you paint in acquerelli? My daughter is artista. She is molto bene.'

I'm trying to keep painting when a woman with legs up to her neck, in the tightest fitting jeans, and with the silkiest, darkest long hair turns up to greet the old man, hugging him and kissing him on both cheeks amid a flood of voluble Italian. The only word I recognise is 'Papa.' She peers at my painting and laughs. Well at least I'm evoking a reaction.

'You should go to the Florence art academy. It is where I am studying'. Her English is impeccable.

'Where did you learn to speak such good English?'

'I went to Cheltenham Ladies' College. I wanted to come home to study my art here. The food is so much better than in England.'

You could have fooled me. She looks like she's never eaten so much as a single sweet or fattening morsel. Whereas me? If I even think of a Guinness, I put on weight. She must be a mind-reader because the next thing she says is 'Come, join us for coffee and a cake. One won't hurt you.'

'Don't mind if I do.'

We stroll over to a table in the shade and her papa orders three coffees three cakes and three amaretto. What a perfectly civilized way to spend my time in Siena.

The old man it transpires isn't so old at all; he has five daughters, which probably explains a lot. From the group photo he produces out of his battered leather wallet, they're all stunningly good looking. Sophia is the middle daughter. She shows me images on her phone of her work, and they're superb; classic to a fault, almost from a different era. I tell her that I sell contemporary art and she says she'll visit next time she's in England. We part on excellent terms and I venture to find another location to paint in. The amaretto's warming effect ought to inspire a masterpiece. Half an hour to lunch though. A sketch will have to do.

I'm really enjoying the routine of this trip; the early starts, lectures, painting, lunching, drinking, dozing, more painting, more drinking, eating and sleeping. Add in learning loads, laughter and lovely locations. What's not to love?

I earn my keep on the eighth day. It's my turn to give a talk on presentation, a simple chat about how to make your art stand out when selling or simply displaying it on one's wall at home. Many artists fail to see beyond the painting. They're too close to the subject and end up using anything handy to frame their hard-worked masterpiece. For that an outside pair of eyes helps; just as even the writer of a masterpiece on gallery management can benefit from a good editor. Luckily no one falls asleep. The sisters titter, and one stands up, 'Excuse me. Would you like to come to our home and sort out all our paintings for us when we get back? We'd make you a rather nice lunch?'

What a nice request. I can do no other than agree.

The afternoon meanders as we head off to the port to paint again. It's such hard work...in a quaintly timeless area where the clock stopped sometime in the 1950's. I pull up my little seat and stare out, taking in the odd chugging fishing boat and the disgruntled gulls demanding their fair share of the catch.

It really is the first time in ages that I've not thought about the gallery for more than five minutes. Shame on me, but I'm so absorbed in painting and the brushes seem to flow on their own, leaving me merely the conductor, watching the image transform on the paper. Victor saunters over, says nothing, and moves away again. Is it rubbish? Who knows? It's the first time he hasn't said anything, constructive or otherwise, about my work.

A long pair of legs emerging from a multi-coloured sarong, slowly and seductively moving towards me, are a definite distraction. The legs speak. 'You are with Victor?'

I find I'm looking up at a six-foot; blue-eyed, dark-haired and stunningly good-looking woman.

'I'm part of his art group. Can I help you?'

'He is ignoring me and I am missing him. Tell him I must see him.' That's disappointing but lucky old Victor!

'And who shall I say is asking?'

'I am Veronica,' and she turns and walks off as coolly as she arrived.

I pack everything away and meet up with the rest of the crew in a little bar on the quayside. We have a quick snifter and a chat, comparing notes as all budding artists do. No. Actually it's more like, *My round, what are you drinking?*

Victor looks lost in thought, making notes in his little battered leather book, when I pull him aside. 'I have regards for you from a lady I met on the front. She said her name's Veronica and she wants to see you...'

I haven't finished talking when a blushing Victor interrupts. 'How do you know Veronica?'

'I don't know her at all. She walked up to me while I was painting and...'

'Right. You've not seen her. Okay? And don't mention her name in front of the group.'

'Mums the word ol' boy. Let's do lunch when we're back in England. You've got to tell me'

'Some things are best kept secret.'

'Really?' I'm smiling now. You see, art, paintings, selling, privacy and juicy bits, all part and parcel of the everyday life of a gallery owner. 'Maybe I should write a book one day, Victor, what do you think?'

I think Victor is not amused. He calls out 'Time to go' and we head off to the jalopy for more food and wine, which you know could become habit forming.

As it's the last evening, we show our achievements and sketches, displaying them propped up on chairs and tables on the patio. It's a great mix of styles and colours. Some are really good. I cannot comment on mine. Liliana serves up drinks and I find myself impelled to make a little speech.

'Ladies and Gents'. Maybe I should say my lords, ladies and other dignitaries, however I digress. 'I'd like on everyone's behalf to thank Victor and all of you for making this a fantastic time. I've enjoyed every second. It's such a change from being in my gallery and so I've decided to make you all one of my special cocktails to celebrate I shall call it a *Tuscan Sunset.*'

I produce, from the carrier bag at my feet, a bottle of gin, a bottle of vodka, a bottle of vermouth a bottle of Drambuie, some pink grapefruit juice and a bottle of grenadine, all secretly purchased earlier in the day. *Tuscan Sunsets* turn out to be smooth and don't taste that strong but don't be fooled my friends; the second one affects the knees and the third illuminates the night sky. Funny really, as nearly everyone in the party manages to drink three of them.

'Good grief ol' boy! You've managed to inebriate the whole group.'

'Well, it should loosen up everyone and after all it's a colourful bit of Tuscan fun.'

Penelope saunters over and sits herself down right beside me. 'This is our last night. Don't you think we should do something frivolous?'

'Any suggestions?'

'Indeed, but not here.'

Victor is holding court and retelling something historical about the area to gales of alcohol-induced laughter.

Penelope whispers in my ear. Is she kidding? I think not.

I excuse myself to step outside for fresh air and to take in the beautiful view. Everything appears to twinkle on the horizon. Must be the fishing boats. I feel an arm around mine.

'I've wanted you since we met at the airport.' It's not Penelope but the headmistress to my shocked surprise. 'You men are all the same. You play it cool knowing deep down what's going on.'

'Honest, we don't.'

'Well it looks like I shall have to show you.' Without hesitation she grabs my hair and pulls me into a kiss full on the lips. I try hard not to respond and she breaks away at last. 'Oh, I'm so sorry. I seem to have allowed myself to be carried away.'

'That's okay. My cocktails have been known to have special after effects.'

'I don't usually kiss strange men.'

'I'm not that strange but I promise not to say a word if you don't.'

She does it again, goes right ahead and plants a smacker on my mouth, then turns around and states 'I'm off to bed.' She brushes past Penelope on the way into the villa.

'Am I missing something?'

'No, I don't think so!'

'Were you snogging that woman? I'm sure I saw you in a rather awkward looking embrace. Really! How common!'

'Penelope, I'm merely a humble gallery owner.'

'Well humble your derriere up to my room right now. That's an order, not a request.' She too turns and leaves.

Well, there go. Two women having beaten their retreat; what else follows? Maybe I should be a gentleman and retire to my own bed? On the other hand, maybe not. Good night.

Breakfast is later than usual and quiet. Everyone is quiet, and Penelope is exceptionally quiet.

'Morning everyone' I try for a lilt of verbal sunshine.

Eventually the day slowly matures and heads reassemble themselves.

Charles taps me on the arm 'What was in those cocktails old boy? You must give me your recipe! Gladys was beside herself.' Charles winks appreciatively.'

'I'm afraid that's a trade secret...but for you I'll write it down. Do be careful though. It has a habit of making people do things they sometimes can't remember.'

'Spot on dear chap. Spot on 'Charles is a reborn Tuscan sun-setter.

Penelope is looking different today. It's not her very chic white, two-piece, linen outfit. It's that she's wearing a wedding ring. She's almost apologetic as she asks, 'May I buy one of your paintings? I love the one of the port you worked on yesterday.'

'It would be my pleasure but please accept it as a gift.' Either Penelope has no taste or I'm not as bad as I think I am. At painting that is.

She notices I've noticed her wedding ring. 'He's an old sod who doesn't care what I do or say. You ought to come and visit us sometime if you're ever in Suffolk.'

'Thanks. I might just surprise you one day.'

Victor pulls me to one side and offers me the opportunity to host an exhibition based on several trips he's made to Venice. I agree, knowing his entourage will follow devoutly and maybe, just maybe, Penelope will come along, minus husband.

We bid our goodbyes back at the dreaded Pisa airport. What a great time I've had. My passion for selling is now reinforced by a greater knowledge of how to paint myself. Life will never be the same again. I wonder when, or indeed if, I'll ever get the chance to paint again.

ULTRAMARINE BLUE

It's half past four and neither wine nor tea, not a drop, has passed my lips all day. Parched is the word that springs to mind.

'Hello may I come in.'

'Certainly, please do.'

She's wearing a plunging V-neck dress, which just shows a hint of leopard-patterned, or it may be cheetah, bra.

'I'm just about to crack a bottle. Fancy a glass?'

'That's very nice. Yes please.'

I produce two Swedish designer glasses and bottle of Rioja from my stock room in which boxes of wine no longer outnumber paintings but be reassured, there's still plenty left. It's just that they now all fit, nicely stacked in the corner.

'Mm this is good,' she says. 'Now, my name's Margo.' She places her expensive looking pink patent handbag on the desk and looks me straight in the eye. 'I'll come right to the point. I can help you and your gallery can help me.'

'Well, that's a good opener. Pray continue.' I pour more wine into our glasses.

'I have a client who wants to launch an unusual website.'

'How unusual?'

'We'd need to black out the windows.'

'And?'

'We'd use a few scantily clad models and for a backdrop we'd love you to put up any art with a nude theme!'

'That's kind of you but what's the benefit to the gallery?'

'There's lots of wealthy clients and you never know.'

I sip my wine, pondering what sort of website she means.

Margo smiles for me. That's fatal 'Can we put a speedboat outside the entrance?'

'Anything else?'

'I can get a Ferrari and an Aston Martin or two to park on the street!'

'Hang on. I'm a gallery not a footballer's playground. How much will your client pay for the evening?'

'Nothing in cash. But we'll provide everything; champagne, girls, a magician, DJ, the lot and you get to go on the website.'

I must be mad! But then as I've found out on more than one occasion, you have to be mad to own an art gallery.

I find myself saying 'Why not?' I still don't know what sort of website she's promoting.

'Fab. Are you free for an early breakfast tomorrow? At seven? It's one of these business breakfast clubs they have there.'

I hate early starts. 'I suppose so.'

'Right. See you at the Grand Hotel tomorrow.' With that she smiles, picks up her bag, turns on her smart designer heels and leaves. Nice pins methinks.

Belinda expresses caution. 'What's that all about? She's after you. You can tell. Did you see the way she flicked her hair? I'd be careful if I was you.'

Thankfully Belinda isn't me and I'm not Belinda. 'Well, there's nothing like a good reception to grab some media interest for the gallery. And no harm having a bit of fun eh! They only want to hire the place for a night.'

'Yes, Boss'. Belinda smiles knowingly, like all true intuitively women learn to do from birth. All I do is own the place. How silly of me to believe I know what's going on in it!

In the hotel lobby I get a professional kiss on both cheeks from Margo who places her arm on mine and steers me over to her client. 'George Lambert, how do you do!'

'I do well above middling thanks.' His hand isn't as large as mine but he's strong and uses the pretext of a handshake to try to crush my knuckles. It's all about animal dominance. Luckily, I know how to lock my upper arm and grip just as hard. My mind is already having second thoughts about him as a client and all the hairs are up on my forearm.

'Come meet Cynthia, my partner in crime,' says George.

Standing by one of the tables is another dangerous-looking individual. A blonde woman. Correction. A peroxide blonde with fake boobs and a facelift that must have cost a fortune. How red are her lips? Dangerously red. She eyes me up and down. 'Margo says you're wonderful!'

'What can I say?' I reply.

'You must come back to ours after breakfast. This is an ungodly hour to gather. I never drink champagne before nine.'

I can't see a wedding ring, but she is flashing enough diamond rings to blind you on a sunny day. I deduce that she's not Mrs. Lambert.

'Sit by me and tell me all about yourself. I'm sure you're not boring.'

'Where would you like me to begin?'

'Are you married?'

'Not that I know of.'

'That's a good start.'

'I own a gallery and...'

She interrupts. 'I know and what else?'

'You're going to hire my gallery for an evening.'

'Are you for hire'

'I'm sorry. Am I for hire? Are you kidding?'

'Not at all. I have friends who'd adore hiring you for an evening.'

It is only twenty past seven. A stupidly early hour to be propositioned. This is without doubt the strangest of breakfast meetings. *She means I could be an escort*. There's a thought. I park it and pour a large coffee. Let's change tactics.

'So, what do you do'?

'I just love to have fun and work as little as possible. I'm a catalyst you could say.'

Umm. All right. Change subjects again. 'How many bods at this reception?'

'Maybe sixty. Give or take a few.'

'We can accommodate that.' I'm trying to sound less apprehensive than I'm now feeling. *Why did I say yes?*

Some bigwig from the Chamber of Commerce calls us to order then and we have to endure a boring talk from a boring man who owns a naval chandlery.

Cynthia smiles. Her botoxed brow doesn't move. 'Some chains are fun but his are way too big. Even I can't imagine things to do with an anchor chain except hang an anchor on it.' A hand squeezes my thigh and Cynthia smiles again. all mock innocence. 'Let's go. The chauffeur's outside and my watch says it's almost time for bubbles.'

Margo, Cynthia, George and yours truly make a quick exit. No time for after chats or business card exchanges. Outside a black stretch Chevrolet with tinted windows is waiting, beside it a chauffeur wearing a smart grey suit and a peaked hat, is holding the rear door open. It's like a scene in a crass, B rated American movie.

Good grief, it gets worse. The interior is furnished in red leather seats with a wood veneer surround. Margo opens a small hatch, extracts a bottle and pours out four glasses of *Veuve Cliquot*.

'Well it is after nine, now. Cheers darlings'

We arrive at what can only be described as a mansion where the gates open automatically and you hear the scrunch of white pebbles under rubber as we slowly drive up to the front door. The place itself is massive and accessed through a pair of

Hammer Horror doors with highly polished brass knockers which are flung open for us by a maid in full uniform.

'Drinks in the lounge Madame?'

'By the pool. It's more relaxing'.

We follow Cynthia over the marble floor to the swimming pool It's like no other place I've ever seen. There are luxurious couches covered in soft satin and two massive chandeliers hanging over the water. The pool has that expensive ultramarine look to it. A wonderful colour.

'They must be Murano. The tiles.'

'Correct. I had them commissioned a year ago.'

We sit at the far end looking out over a magnificent garden. Crass has morphed into class. 'Wow, it's beautiful. Do you have many sculptures dotted around out there?'

She doesn't answer because the maid appears with a silver tray of smoked salmon blinis and, you guessed it, more champagne.

Margo is sitting chatting to George and Cynthia says exactly what I'm thinking; 'Nobody should do seven am! I'm exhausted' Then she downs her entire glass in one. 'Can you swim?' she holds her arm out for the glass to be refilled.

'Not often enough.'

'Why don't you have a go? I'll join you.'

I protest 'I didn't come prepared. No shorts.'

'No need, house rules. Nobody swims in anything but what nature provides.' She stands up. Strips off and dives in. Artificial or not, she has an excellent physique.

Margo follows suit but George walks off talking into his mobile phone. 'Come on grumpy drawers. Get in!' shouts Margo.

When in Rome as the saying goes. Clothes off and splash. At least my suit's not getting ruined this time. I'm in an indoor pool with not one but two naked ladies. What can I say?

'What's the website all about then?' That's aimed generally at either or both women. Distraction technique.

'Shhhh! This isn't work time. Bubbles required!'

The maid appears with another bottle to top up the glasses. George is nowhere to be seen. Margo swims right up to me brushing her body against mine. 'Said we'd be good for each other, didn't I?'

Cynthia is sipping her champagne by the edge of the pool. 'What would you like to do next?'

'Well in truth I really should be going. You know gallery to run and all that.'

'Why don't you stay for lunch?'

'I really should go. Ladies it's been a delight but art calls.'

Cynthia just says, 'Don't be so prissy. Lunch is going to be served at twelve-thirty Then you can go if you must.'

It's a tough call. What should I do? Looks like I'm going to be late for work.

CHARTREUSE

A young lady pops her head around the door. 'Excuse me. Please will you have a look at my dad's work. He doesn't live too far from here? It wouldn't take long. You see, he never leaves the house and the place is stuffed to the gills. It's good stuff, I think. Please would you?'

An unusual approach for sure and intriguing. 'I will. With pleasure.' Sounds like something I shouldn't miss. 'I'll pop over later this afternoon. How's that?'

'Smashing. I'll tell him'

I love impromptu occasionally and today is an impromptu sort of day especially as Belinda's in a tidying and rearranging mood.

'I'm off to see a reclusive artist.'

'That makes a change. What is it about artists? Why aren't any of them normal?'

'And your point is?'

'The gallery is a magnet for odd bods, you know. It's a bit like a selection of my ex boyfriends. Just saying.'

'Young lady! It's what makes the art world rotate and besides I know you still love it. You could always be a stock broker.'

'Not bloody likely!'

Time to leave. Belinda is unimpressed and likely to stay that way.

The address I've been given isn't exactly just round the corner. It's a few miles away to be precise and getting there takes longer than it should because I'm held up en-route by not one but two separate funeral cortèges. The countryside is obviously bad for health and longevity these days. To cap it off I end up behind a refuse wagon and nothing and nobody is more important to our bin men than slinging green and brown plastic wheelie bins around to cause as much havoc as possible.

The bell doesn't work.

I knock hard on the old, blue-painted, wooden door. After a while the door opens and a head appears. A pair of beady eyes looks me up and down. 'I'm not sure I want to let you in.'

I could just turn around and leave to satisfy his insecurity but instead I tell him I'm here because his daughter pleaded with me to come. 'She said your paintings are worth the journey. So, can I see them, if only to satisfy her.' That does the trick. Graham opens the door fully and backs away. Entering the hallway, I'm confronted with loads of stacked canvases. There's a narrow path to the kitchen and an old kettle with the red whistling top is merrily boiling away.

'Cuppa?'

Progress in the trust stakes. 'I'll have a glass of water if you don't mind. How long have you been painting?

'About twenty years, give or take.'

'Let's have a look then. Where shall we start?'

'Upstairs?' We climb to the landing to be confronted with hundreds more canvases, all stacked on top of each other.

'How many have you painted?'

'Quite a few, I guess.'

It's obvious he's been constrained only by a total lack of space. The two bedrooms are full to the ceilings and the bathroom has a stack in it too. It seems the landing will have to serve as a viewing area. Graham sort of sidles into the first bedroom and then suddenly there's a crash followed by a certain expletive and a white Persian cat races through my legs and shoots down the stairs looking positively guilty. Well that would explain the cat hairs sticking on more than a few on the paintings.

'It's so fine and it sticks to the varnish all the time,' explains Graham.

Distracted I'm peering out of the window. There's a shed out there, sadly looking like it's seen better days. 'Is that your studio?'

'It was, but it's pretty rotten so I don't use it now...and all my trains are out there in boxes.'

I decide not to pursue the benefits of having a Tri-ang train set tootling round the studio whilst blissfully painting away.

Graham excavates six canvases, holding them precariously balanced on the banister rail. 'This is one of my least favourite pieces.'

Why show it to me then? I don't say that aloud because it's brilliantly wacky, a naïve, colourful, figurative picture on a garish, chartreuse background. Two glaring eyes haunt the middle ground, in the face of a David Bowie lookalike – apart from being bald.

'Not exactly a user-friendly colour, is it?'

'I got it cheap in a church bazaar a while back.'

His strange, humorous, almost alien, figures emerge as the theme of most of the paintings. His colours are bold and certainly different. 'I think you'll scare the public. I love them, but you need to clean them up and defuzz them.'

Three hours have passed, and we're still working our way through the upstairs paintings. I can't see any more; my head is clogged full of new images. The best thing to do is arrange to call again to view the contents of the downstairs collection another day.

'Well, I would like to show your work in my gallery.'

'If you say so.' Graham isn't showing signs of positivity or great joy. Sometimes I feel I shouldn't bother. All in a day's work, though, dealing with negativity and cynicism.

The following week I plough through another two hundred or so canvases and eventually select a grand total of thirty-six.

'Who on earth do you think will buy my work?'

'That is my gamble and my department. I really believe they will sell.' As I'm loading the car though I'm wondering if this might be a challenge too far.

I pull up outside the gallery and Belinda and Charlie assist with the unloading.

'He's weird' says Belinda

'Has he got a woman?' asks Charlie 'I bet he's a bit, you know...kinky.'

'To be honest, we never discussed his sex life. Why don't you ring him up and ask him, eh?'

'Ooh! Who got out of bed the wrong side then?' Those ten days in Tuscany already seem a light year away.

'Sorry, ladies. Drinks on me when we close up.'

'Agreed,' they reply in unison.

A woman's' perspective is very important in art and on reflection their first opinion of Graham's work rings alarm bells. Good grief, I'm beginning to listen to others. How refreshing. My dream team decides they like two thirds of the work and their suggestions for what to do with the rest contain several repeated expletives. I listen and agree with their selection and reasoning.

With the day's done, we lock up and head to the wine bar. My girls - correction, the staff - never forget a promise. The wine is poured and the day slows into chill mode.

'Well, did anyone miss me while I was out?'

'Didn't notice you'd gone' laughed Charlie

'Who are you anyway?' Belinda clinks my glass with hers.

'Cheers.'

For once I realise I'm seriously tired, physically and mentally, and we've several large shows ahead plus Victor's Venetian show we've now added to the calendar. The waiter arrives at our table and asks if we'd like anything else. There's only one answer in the circumstances. 'Another bottle of the same please, and a jug of water.' At least water is good for you.

PAYNE'S GREY

Payne's Grey is a very useful and a very dangerous colour. Just the smallest amount does wonders but use it to excess and the blackness in it is damning and ruins everything.

Mrs. Topping is on the phone. She's wailing and shouting out nearly simultaneously. We're a gallery, not a domestic abuse help-line. From what I gather between the sobs and tirades, Mr. Topping has been a naughty boy. How naughty it's not for me to say, but apparently the nude painting over the bed is causing a lot of stress in Mrs. Toppings life.

'He's always staring at her. I originally bought it from you thinking he'd love it but that bitch has taken over our lives. He's obsessed with her.'

I try to calm her down, saying it's only a painting. Apparently, that's entirely the wrong thing to say.

'No, it's not,' she wails. 'I've met her. He's bloody well having an affair with her.'

How can anyone have an affair with a painting? I manage not to say that to her.

'He decided to take up life drawing. There she was in his class. That bitch is over our head in our bedroom and he's shagging her senseless.' There's a momentary silence and then an enormous crash of glass followed by further wailing.

'Hello! Hello! Mrs. Topping, are you alright?'

The phone is picked again and she says, 'I've done it. Smashed the little whore to pieces. I'm so sorry for the trouble. I just had to speak to someone.'

'Are you okay?' I hope I sound as concerned as I feel I should.

'I've broken the painting...hic. Do you think it could be repaired?'

Apparently, the truth is she's as drunk as a skunk and jealous as hell of a mere painting. As I say, it's not my role to judge anyone and I like to think that I show genuine concern for the people I meet in my business capacity. Mrs. Topping is crying down the phone and no man likes to hear a woman cry. It upsets us beyond belief.

'Why don't you come in and have a nice glass of something special next time you're in town.'

'Oh yes. Thank you. Good idea. We'll come in later.'

I didn't mean today. Oh God! 'Do you mean with Mr. Topping?'

'Me and Mr. Topping's credit card and my bestie, Lucy.' Her mood has changed completely. Methinks it's time to batten down the hatches and prepare for war. I mean I'm an old-fashioned romantic at heart. I like the world to be nice and peaceful. I'm not into violence and disharmony, and the Topping conversation has genuinely upset my psyche.

'Are you alright Boss?' Belinda enquires.

'I'm a bit shook up with Mrs. Topping's drunken battle cries and woes down the phone. She's bloody jealous of a painting.'

Belinda heads off to the kitchen, returning with the glass of red wine she knows I desperately need. Bright girl, our Belinda. I drink it down in one.

'I'll never figure out the female race.'

'You're not supposed to,' Belinda chuckles. 'Let me handle her when she arrives'

'With pleasure.'

We spend the next hour sorting the catalogue for Bruce's show. 'What do you think we should call it?' I ask.

'Willies on parade.' We both break into peals of laughter.

'No, seriously.'

We eventually settle on a title, after half-heartedly exploring *Hard and Soft, It's all in the dangle,* and best of all, *Let me paint your...*

The title of the show is to be *Trust.*

Belinda assembles the images; she's good on the computer, unlike myself, who hasn't the foggiest idea which buttons to press.

Time flies and Mrs. Topping and Lucy walk in. dressed to kill. Literally.

'Good afternoon, ladies. You look like you're on a mission.'

Mrs. Topping is dressed in a smart dark grey suit with the tightest three-quarter length trousers and high heels. Payne's Grey at its best.

Lucy is in rather too tight a blouse and blue flared culottes. She's teetering on a pair of severely dangerous high heels.

'I'm so sorry about before, it was most unprofessional of me.'

'As long as you're alright, Mrs. Topping.'

'Call me Tina. I've told you before,' There's a smile cracking her well made up face. Belinda takes control, producing a bottle of fizz.

'Thank you my dear. I want something different above my bed. There's room for something special there now.'

Belinda offers Tina a chair beside the computer screen and shows her some of Bruce's paintings. The girl has a wicked sense of humour and before long Tina Topping finds one she loves. 'That will show him. Just look at those thighs. Makes me want him right now,' she says, in an undertone.

I suppose if Mr. T. turns out to be bisexual, he might like it too. Keep schtum on that thought.

'I want it. When can I have it?'

'The work arrives next Tuesday for the exhibition opening on Thursday.'

'Well its mine. Can I have it delivered on Friday?'

Belinda writes the order and, bless her, asks for a credit card.

'How much shall I put through?'

'All of it,' says Mrs Topping. 'How much is it?'

Belinda looks at me helplessly.

'It will be up at ten and a half but for you Tina, we'll say nine thousand.'

'That's perfect, and I want that beautiful glass piece on the table too. It's a rainbow and I feel like I've found the crock of gold. My grandfather was Irish you know. Drank himself to death on Poteen.'

'The Irish have a lot to answer for then. Distilled potatoes is only good for arthritis, one of my uncles used to say.'

'How about another glass of bubbly?'

I'm happy to play barman this time.

Lucy picks up a glass bowl and holds it up to the light. 'You don't mind if I touch it?'

'Not at all.'

'I love the way the light bursts through and the cuts are superb. This would look so good on my dining room table.'

Before I can say anything, Tina says, 'Add it to my bill.'

'Don't be silly, Tina, 'I couldn't possibly.'

Oh yes, she can. Neither Belinda nor I say a word. We let the two ladies fight it out. Luckily for us it takes mere seconds to reach a blissful conclusion and the piece is added to the bill.

Tina places her hand on my shoulder and gives it a squeeze. 'Will you come and deliver my painting for me?'

'It will be my pleasure,' I assure her

The two ladies leave in a far more jovial mood than they arrived in. *What's that expression? Retail therapy.*

'Well that's one willy down. Nineteen more to go,' says Belinda in a jubilant mood.

'Well done that girl' I say.

This really is a great way to start a show and the work hasn't even arrived yet. It does next day in two huge crates deposited outside the front door just as I arrive to open up. The crates contain enough wooden boards to make a garden shed, I reckon. Armed with my trusty electric screwdriver, I unscrew at least two hundred brass screws. Slowly but surely the containers release their goodies. Bruce has packed the paintings magnificently with each canvas wrapped first in shrink-wrap film and then in bubble-wrap. They take forever to unwrap but eventually the contents lay spread out around the gallery leaning against my skirting boards.

Without a shadow of a doubt, this is going to be a very different exhibition to anything else I've ever shown. And *showing* is definitely the word for a room with twenty naked men, even if, in fact, each picture is of the same man.

By the time Charlie and Belinda arrive for work, I've managed to hang half the show. 'No comments please, it's too early.' Charlie seems genuinely fascinated while Belinda looks somewhat ambivalent.

The whole show is hung within an hour of opening up, apart from a spot of tidying up here and there. A few sculptures to dot around and the gallery will be ready. All we need now is a lot of luck, a lot of red dots placed on paintings and a damn good opening night. I've been very selective with my invitations this time, as our sponsors have already asked quite a few of their clients and acquaintances.

Thursday. Bruce walks in at midday.

I wait for his comments on my hanging.

'I think they read well,' he nods in approval. First hurdle over. Now we wait for the opening bash.

There is always a sense of panic to any show we put on. I mean you just never know who'll come, in spite of the RSVPs so catering and liquid refreshments are a guessing game. At least this time the champagne is arriving by the box load, and Bruce's wine merchant and part-time model has donated forty bottles of Alicote from his own vineyard.

Freddy Mark II arrives in a fluster. 'I have the stickers for the bubbly; we need to stick them over the labels as the wine merchants have slipped up. You don't mind doing it, do you? I'm so busy! See you later.' He spins and dashes out the door. That's all we need, fifty bottles to be relabelled, Rock n roll.

The wheels begin to turn. The caterers arrive and set up, and I have to ask them to move as they're taking up too much space on the floor.

The caterer argues 'We need four trestles.'

The owner of the gallery is adamant. 'You can't have them. Two's the max. This isn't a bloody garden fete!' I'm feeling the pressure obviously.

Belinda and Charlie disappear to get ready, leaving Bruce and I, to cope, before any further storm hits.

'Good luck with my show, I wouldn't trust anyone else to put this on.'

'Thanks for the vote of confidence' I reply, sitting down for the first time all day.

There's a knock on the front door and I look up to see a tall, bearded chap wearing a red-sequined ball gown, blocking the entrance. 'What time is kick off, sweetie?'

'It's seven,' I say, unfazed.

'Oh bugger. We're early.'

I think he's expecting me to let him stay, but my tradition is to allow no one in till just before an event starts. 'I'm very sorry. We have to close up for a while to finalise everything, but we look forward to seeing you again soon.' I lock the door and switch off half the lighting. Big beard doesn't object, luckily, and strolls off with his little friend, who's in a shocking purple suit, arm in arm.

Bruce changes his attire in the kitchen. He re-enters wearing a golden-silk, Indian style jacket with black satin trousers. I think we need Oscar Wilde to complete this scene. Freddy Mark II and his partner, Derek, arrive in matching, pale-blue suits, brightly coloured shirts and cravats. I'm keeping it simple, like Johnny Cash, sporting a black suit, black shirt and black dress shoes.

Belinda walks in wearing a full-length dress with just a hint of cleavage showing and a red scarf that matches her lipstick. Charlie is in loud mode, but something inside me says she won't be as loud as some of the guests. She has on a bright yellow jacket, white blouse and matching yellow skirt, longer than normal but still above her knees, finished off with very high, golden heels.

Bring it on; the gallery team are dressed to impress!

The guests start to arrive and it's more akin to a Hollywood red-carpet event. I've never seen so much sparkle, especially on the men. Suffice it to say the artwork is competing with the guests for attention. For once I don't know most of the guests so it's a bit like being at a distant friend's wedding However, there is one fundamental difference because this wedding is all about selling Bruce's male nudes to over-dressed men in OTT makeup and, in several cases, ball gowns.

There are some women too, mostly with the obligatory short spiky hair. The photographer is beside himself, trying not to focus on anything too risqué as his newspaper is read by *everyday folk*. Where's the Sun or Mirror when you want them?

Champagne flows and the noise levels rise with laughter, coarse and hilarious. Nobody seems to recognise Antoine, then subject of Bruce's paintings, when he arrives in a very smart woollen jacket, pink striped shirt and black slacks with loafers, looking dead normal. It's because he's dressed. I think that's for the best in this crowd.

Within minutes the place is packed, the canapés are consumed and the bottles are emptying at a record rate.

Belinda bumps into me, 'It's madness, total chaos. How am I supposed to sell anything?'

'Stay calm. Just wait till Bruce says a few words.' I try to sound convincing.

Freddy Mark II takes the microphone. 'Shut up you lot I can't hear myself think.'

The place goes silent. Let me hand you over to my partner, Derek Audrey.'

So that's his surname. Audrey. I didn't know it till this moment.

Derek now takes centre stage to deliver a short but blue comedy routine, to rapturous applause, before declaring the show open and introducing Bruce as the star of the show. More cheers and then Bruce is standing there in total silence in front of everyone.

He takes a gentle cough. 'Trust is something we all need in our lives. I paint to survive and survive by painting. My relationship with wine I trust to my dear friend and my own taste buds. My trust in art is with this gallery and I trust you enjoy what is displayed and acquire some. Right now. I trust it's to your taste and I humbly thank you all for coming here tonight.'

There's a huge cheer and rapturous applause.

A man in with a fairly reserved dress code taps my arm. 'I want this one. It so reminds me of you, love'. He means the chap beside him in a blue dress with long satin gloves, not me. Red dot number two. To my considerable pleasure several more paintings are snapped up in a flurry of red dots.

The champagne is certainly flowing. Charlie looks frustrated at being unable to find a man to pounce on and Belinda is chatting to two women who look like they're both hitting on her. She still manages to place a red dot on one of the smaller paintings for them. Good girl.

Eleven-fifteen and all the champagne is gone. Mr. Audrey strolls over. 'What a lovely evening, darling. We've so enjoyed our little soiree. We're going to move down to the club for the after party. You simply must come. Bruce and Antoine are coming. Bring the girls too.'

What can I say? *What a great idea.* Not! 'We'd love to. I'll just check if Belinda and Charlie can make it.'

No points for guessing their answer.

'Yay,' says Charlie. 'Party time.'

'Count me in,' says Belinda.

The crowd disperses rather quickly, allured by the pull of more booze down the road. Bruce is sitting sipping a large glass of wine and looking a touch perplexed.

'What's up, matey?'

'I was thinking maybe I shouldn't have sold these so quickly. I'm never going to revisit this series again.'

There's no pleasing some folk; I want to throttle him. It's been the most delicate and difficult exhibition to mount, which, in case he hasn't noticed, has been a magnificent success. There are only four paintings left unsold and it's not even day one proper yet.

'Let's go join the party. I'm sure you'll feel better soon.'

'I suppose so. Antoine enjoyed the evening.'

We lock up, leaving the battle ground mess behind and hail a taxi. I have to admit to bailing out of the ensuing party at about two in the morning, leaving them all to it. Bruce is dancing away, Charlie has a crowd around her and Belinda is still being chatted up by the same two women. Only Antoine is nowhere to be seen.

As I'm leaving, a silver haired gent eyes me up 'Are you with your wife?'

'I'm not married.'

'Who's that then?'

He's the artist. We've just had an opening at my gallery.

'You're not a couple then?'

'No. I could say I'm his dealer, but I don't like that terminology.'

'Fancy lunch sometime this week?'

Heavens above, I'm being chatted up. 'Sorry, I hate to disappoint you, I bat for the other side.'

'Don't knock it till you try it dearie!' Deja-vu. This is like the man at the party in London. *What vibe am I putting out?*

'Here's my card if you ever fancy...'

'And here's mine if you ever fancy some art for your home.'

I walk out into the early hours of the morning and hail a cab'

'Taxi!!' I'm going home alone. Thank God.

COOL WHITE

Graham's work is selling rather better than I anticipated. So much so that it doesn't seem out of the ordinary when a chap walks in showing great interest in one of the pieces, although he talks just a bit too fast and his eyes are dancing round his head. I'm no expert on drugs, but I'd be inclined to suspect cocaine's involved.

In short after forcing me to listen to a shed load of musical management bullshit at double speed, he says he wants to use Graham's work for his all new female rock band. There's one painting in particular in which fingers are entering the eye sockets in the skull.

'This will make a fantastic cover for the new single. It's called *Not My Eyes*. Man, you should hear them. Fuckin' awesome.'

'Okay. How much would you like to pay for the right to use the image'

'It'll be great PR for you and the gallery and I'm sure the dude would love to see his name on a disc.'

'Don't think so. You can buy the painting and a licensing fee for commercial use of the image.'

'I can use another painting from another gallery.'

'But you like this artist.'

'Alright. Fuck it. How much?'

We don't haggle long and he hands me an Amex card.

'Fancy a drink? Seal the deal.'

'Do you have Jack Daniels?

'Wine or coffee?'

'I'm not much of a drinker. Okay. Glass of red.'

'With pleasure'. Hope he calms down. I'm feeling the stress of his treble speed conversation and wired thought processes.

He sits down to quaff the wine, head slowly turning left and right, looking around the room, humming.

'We could do a photo shoot in here; it's got a nicely faded feel

'I beg your pardon?'

'Yeah man. I mean a coat of paint and a few mirrors and - voila, show time!'

'Nice thought but I'm not really looking to change things. I like my gallery the way it looks.'

He downs the wine in one. 'Ten grand man; think about it.' He stands and walks out the door. He's back five minutes later. 'Forgot the painting, man.'

Belinda's stayed out the way the whole time and reappears only when the coast is clear.

'What was that all about?'

'Some bloke just bought a painting and told me to repaint the gallery.'

'Well it is looking a bit shabby.'

This isn't what I want to hear. Is no one on my side? Although, looking around, I have to admit a lick of paint wouldn't go amiss. You get used to your surroundings and if it takes a coked-up customer to point it out...Bugger!

The next day the cokehead's on the phone. 'Dude, I've been thinking!'

'Hey, that's great. So have I.'

'The record company will pay 15k if you let them use your gaff. They only need it for a couple of days. What do you say?'

'What colour would you like the walls painted?'

'Deep red and black.' He waits a micro-second for my gasp. 'Nah, kidding. A cool white will do.'

I takes me two milli-seconds to decide. 'Done. When?'

'Monday.'

Square it with Belinda and Charlie. 'Ladies, we need to clear the gallery for a few days.'

'Why?' asks Charlie?

'When?' asks Belinda.

'Saturday. It won't take long.'

Why am I doing this? Ah yes, fifteen grand. That's why. Lick of paint time and a film crew coming in on Monday There's a degree of mental resistance but I even know a client who can paint the place on Sunday. So why make excuses to avoid the achievable?

The weekend traverses without any glitches despite Belinda announcing she has to finish at six-thirty 'Coz I've got a date and need to get ready.'

'Fine' I smile 'We'll finish before then, wont we?' And we do, just.

With true Rock 'n' roll timing, nobody from the band or label arrive on the Monday till eleven and even then, it takes six large coffees from some unmentionable coffee chain to get things underway.

Did I forget to say I'm a coffee snob?

The band arrives looking like they've just been let out of school for the day but, after a mere twenty minutes of makeup, lights, action, reappear in slashed leather and black lace demonic outfits, ready and able to attack a host of zombies, and to save a poor, lost, virgin soldier who, according to the shooting script, needs a good sorting out.

In actuality, the girls are all really sweet and polite. Unlike the camera crew, who couldn't give a toss about my gallery or the subject matter of the film so long as they get paid. Just an observation.

To my considerable surprise the reclusive Graham breaks his habitual shyness to come into town today of all days. He walks in to find one of his paintings blown up and replicated six times around the room and filming in full swing.

'I wanted a word with you.'

'Sure thing. Let's go round the back.'

'I don't think I can cope with all this.

'My dear chap, it's all good exposure. What would you rather do, leave them all in your house piled up for ever more?'

'I hate them all. I want to destroy them now.'

Great. If that's how you feel, let me get you a knife and you can shred away. See if I care. But do let them finish filming first. The band sound really good.'

By the look on his face, I know he's deadly serious, so I take him through to the stock room and get him a Stanley knife. Guess what? He slashes each of the paintings leaning against the wall. He's actually enjoying himself and getting in the mood I suggest he puts his head through like an old Edwardian pier mock-up and take a photo, for posterity. Although a bloody gun might have been more useful than a camera. There we are surrounded by ripped up canvases and broken wooden stretchers. 'I trust you're going to tidy up and throw this bloody mess out?'

'I feel much better, honestly. It's been bugging me since you came to my house'. The sweat is pouring down his face.

Why do I bother? Graham, you're a total fruitcake.'

'I promise I'll paint you more - far better than this lot of rubbish'

'I wait with baited breath.'

Out in the gallery, the girls are still miming to their forthcoming new release and life goes on as per any normal Monday on planet Earth.

'Mate!' The director looks in my direction.

I hate being called that. 'Do you mean me by any chance?'

'Yeah, whatever your name is. I want another stiff and you'll do seeing as you're doing nothing. Make up! Tart him up!'

I can see the tabloid-heading now; *Gallery owner prematurely deceased in own shop.*

But why not? Graham's destroyed his work and I'm seething inside. Within minutes, I'm a dead carcass.

'Lie there now and don't move till I tell you. Got it?'

Think of the money.

The gallery looks very different lying on the floor. The girls look rather taller from down here too. Then they strut over and each of them positions a foot on my torso. Okay, so now I'm a stiff with eyes glazed over, enjoying the view.

'Cut. Perfect. That's a wrap.' The director looks pleased with himself. There you go, I'm immortalised and all in one take. I doubt anyone would believe what's happened today.

When they've all cleared out and gone, the place is quiet again and Graham returns to talk to me. 'I'm sorry about what happened before.'

'You know what Graham, I've risen from the dead and guess what? I just don't care.'

INDIGO

Indigo and its depth works a treat for night paintings. It's dark and occasionally sultry, like the woman who paints mysterious nocturnal abstracts with bright yellow city lights.

There's a definite relationship between the work of the female artists I meet and their height. The shorter they are, the larger the paintings. This is certainly true for Samantha. Her voice is gravel, pure sex down the phone, and she stands a good four foot three inches depending on which way the wind blows.

She lives with her chap who is jealous of anyone, particularly male, who talks to her, so you'll understand what it's like when I want to visit her studio.

I originally espied her work hanging in a little framer's shop. He has a cupboard – sorry, a bijou studio he uses to show paintings by local artists. There was something intriguing about her work that I liked. So, I ring her up, and arrange to see her.

At a front door, which has seen better days, I'm met by a bloke who's roughly shaved - hardly designer stubble, more unkempt, greasy hair stuck to his scalp like an old mop. His image is reinforced by tatty, worn-out jeans. I take an instant dislike to him and he looks at me like I'm his life-long enemy.

'Is Samantha in?'

'Why?'

'I have an appointment to see her work.'

'I'll check she wants to see you.'

I sense a huge problem. I'm not wrong. 'You have ten minutes. She's over in that room.' He points along the ripped wallpaper of the corridor. I slide past him, stepping over quantities of non-matching shoes and wellies and a sleeping dog and land outside a brown-stained wooden door. I Knock quite hard and turn the sticky Bakelite handle.

Samantha's kneeling on all fours on the floor, her derriere in a very tight pair of jeans facing me as I walk in. What a pleasant greeting. She's painting on a square canvas and her hands are covered in indigo paint.

'Hello Samantha. Who's the bodyguard?'

'You've met Robin then. Don't mind him'. What a voice. She stops and rises up to her full diminutive height.

'Do you smoke?' That would explain things.

'No,' she says. 'I gave up cigarettes years ago. Just little spliffs now and then'. Her voice is down in the dungeon. It's almost a growl with a purring undertone thrown in for good measure.

Hanging off nails are a number of unfinished paintings, with as much paint on the wall as on the canvases. Little sketches on lined notepaper are stuck with drawing pins onto the plaster and an old Dansette record player is spinning *Wild Things Run Fast*. I know it well. I own a copy of the album too. 'Love Joni Mitchell.'

'Me too.' She changes gear and subject. 'How does your gallery work?'

'Rather well apparently!'

'I've been stung before; down in London'

'I don't believe any of my artists have ever had a reason to complain. I pay everyone.'

'That's comforting.' She gets back down on the floor and continues to paint. Watching her in action is almost hypnotic.

I sit myself down on the floor cross-legged. There are no chairs in the room. We just chat away and she continues to paint. Suddenly there's the door loudly bangs open and Robin storms in. 'What the hell do you think you're doing?' His anger is clearly directed at me.

'Conversing. Why?'

Without warning he stomps over and kicks the record player. The stylus makes a loud screech as it skids off the disc and crashes with the player to the floor.

'That's my favourite record, you bastard!'

'Screw you, bitch!' He grabs a jar of murky blue paint-clogged water and hurls it at the wall. Jackson Pollack, eat your heart out! It splashes everywhere, missing me by a few millimetres.

I refuse to engage and fight, which clearly is what he wants. 'I like Joni Mitchell. That's a great album you've ruined.'

Samantha is sobbing curled up in a foetal position and my calm further fans the flames. 'I don't want you in this fucking house! You can't have her!'

Before I can think of a suitable reply, Samantha leaps off the floor and jumps on him, screaming and pulling at his hair.

'I love you when you're angry, you bitch' Astonishingly that's from Robin, laughing hysterically whilst spinning and banging into the wall. Samantha doesn't let go. She continues hitting him, screaming as she does so.

Breaking free, he runs out, down the corridor, kicking the sleeping dog and slamming the front door on his way out.

'I'm so sorry.' She flicks her hair back and wipes her eyes, smearing indigo over her cheeks. 'We divorced years ago and he won't let go.'

'Are you sure you're okay?'

You see you never know what's been going on behind the surface of a painting. Some people just look and say, *That's nice. That'll suit our lounge.* Do they think about the life of the artist? I doubt it. Not unless the artist is about to die and escalate the value of his or her work. Buyers are mercenary bastards. Well here's a case of beautiful paintings, deep, sultry and powerful, the camouflage for a woman being mentally and physically abused by her ex-husband.

Samantha looks up at me and her eyes are full of sorrow. At the same time, they're very beautiful. 'What am I supposed to do?' she asks. Then she kisses me...on the nose.

'Let's have some fun. I know, let's go for a walk. The park's just across the way.' She wipes her hands on a multi-coloured, terry towel, and throws it down on the floor. 'Come on slowcoach!'

We stroll across the road and turn left into one of the last of this country's proper Edwardian style parks with its tidy flowerbeds, exploding in a colourful array of carefully matched flowers. Over in the distance is a bowling green actually in use by a gaggle of elderly ladies and gents. *Hurrah for England.*

Samantha runs off like a mental afghan hound unleashed, hair flying everywhere as she leaps and skips laughing out loud. I sort of meander in the general direction of her wake and stop to watch the octogenarian bowls tournament.

Samantha arrives back at my side. 'When was the last time you made love outside?'

'Not for a long while and just for the record, I've never played bowls either.' It seems the disarmingly right thing to say.

She has rosy cheeks and a beaming smile of happiness, 'I feel like I've been set free, thank you.'

'I don't believe I've done anything untoward apart from viewing your work.'

'Silly boy. You're exactly what I need, right now.'

Technically speaking, Samantha isn't one of my artists. Not yet. Neither is she staff, so normal rules don't apply. There's just one simple set of questions to be addressed. Would she like me to sell her art or not? Would I like to sell her work or not? Would I want to miss an opportunity for some fun? Ah that solitary word, fun. *Would it be fun?*

YELLOW OCHRE

There's a debate that contrasts yellow ochre with raw sienna. Actually, it's more or less the same colour in oils but one is opaquer in watercolours, assuming you care to know that? Anyway Venice, as an artist's playground, has a lot of washed out colours and yellow ochre figures to a great extent.

Or should that be raw sienna?

Victor wants his Venetian show in October and of course

October is when Belinda's planning on leaving the gallery. Time to look for a new member of staff. It dawns on me that I have no more than six weeks to find someone new.

'Belinda! Pardon me for asking, but when exactly in October are you going?'

Belinda bursts into tears. 'I don't want to talk about it now.'

'That's all well and good but I really need to know. We've got Victors exhibition coming up and you've been brilliant and I'm beside myself and I really need to know if it's the beginning or end.'

'It's neither. I changed my mind. They cancelled the course. I don't want to go and I thought you meant you were pleased you were getting rid of me.'

'Are you kidding.' *Women!* 'That's great news; I mean, I'm really sorry it hasn't worked out for you. I want you to stay. Would a pay rise cheer you up?'

I can't begin to tell her how relieved I am. Joyous in fact.

Even if none of us is actually indispensable, great members of staff do make your life so much easier. I'm deeply relieved by Belinda's news.

'Well then, I'm putting you in charge of the show. The whole shebang. So that's it, start now. Catalogue by the weekend please and you choose which image we use for the theme.'

The subject is closed. Belinda appears as relieved as I am. That's retail my dears. It's just like relationships; it's all about communication.

The phone rings. It's Victor. 'My dear chap. Do you need an extra member of staff? My niece, Abigail, needs a month's work placement as part of her university degree. Wouldn't it be fun, if she could help at my show?' He's either weirdly tuning in to my operating frequency or it's the most useful of coincidences.

'Victor ol' boy, tell her to ring me. Belinda is going to look after all the exhibition details and I dare say she'd enjoy having a personal assistant.'

I put the phone down as two elderly ladies, very smartly dressed and what you might call proper, stroll into the gallery. 'Good morning ladies; may we offer you tea or coffee?'

'Are you the young man that owns this establishment?'

'I believe that I do.'

'Good. My name is Woodridge. This is Emily, she is my sister and a wonderful artist and I believe you should inspect her work.'

'How do you do, Emily.' Emily quietly shakes my hand. There's an air of mischief in her deep blue eyes.

'I have some photographs here in my handbag if you would like to see some?'

'With pleasure.'

What I see is unexpected. The photos depict bold landscapes, quite naïve but full of energy. They're simply divine. I fall in love with the quality of the colours. 'If you don't mind me saying, these are brilliant. I love them.'

Emily blushes. 'You won't mess me around, will you? My last boyfriend was an incorrigible flirt and it upset me so.'

'Emily, I don't mix pleasure with business unless it involves a glass of wine or two. May I offer you both a drink?'

'Do you have Cinzano?' The older Miss Woodridge pipes up.

'We might indeed. At the back of the fridge.'

Charlie picks up on the hint straight away and nips out to buy a bottle. She returns quickly and steps out from the kitchen with two iced drinks of the requested tipple. Always ready to please. Not difficult to achieve, given a local wine shop, three doors from the gallery. A Godsend.

We all clink glasses and formality merrily melts way.

We sort out a date for me to visit Emily's studio and as they stand to leave, Emily's sister leans in to me and says, 'Young man. Do you think you might manage to play something a little more classical in your gallery next time we visit?'

'Grateful Dead or Glenn Miller? I quietly respond.'

'Schubert would do nicely.' With that they leave without another word, Emily towed by her Sergeant-Major of a sister.

'How about that then?'

'Aren't they sweet. I'd kill for that art deco brooch Emily was wearing.'

I love being surprised, in a nice way and more times than most it's the older artists that are full of them. However, there's one drawback. Although young at heart, they're an aging collection of wonderful characters and the inevitable is bound to happen sooner or later. We can't play God though and serious art buyers are only too aware of the fact and always seems to want to know how old an artist is. Maybe I should put born and expected to die dates on the labels. Greed you see, I don't like it. I remember lending a painting to a couple who were umming and ahhing about a particular piece. I said to hang it on their walls over the weekend and see if it suited. No obligation. Unfortunately, on the Sunday afternoon I had a phone call from the artist's wife to say he'd died and she wanted all the available work back, obviously expecting an explosion in his market value. I seemed debateable whether the piece I'd lent was available or not. I suppose it was but on the Monday morning I rang the couple to see if they had decided to keep or return the painting. Luckily for them they did want it and agreed to pay for it by credit card there and then. Only then because they loved the picture not the prospect of monetary gain did I reveal that the artist had died the day before.

Back in presentsville, Charlie sits down beside me at the desk. 'I've been thinking! You were so nice to those ladies. In fact, you're really such a sweetie, I think we'd make a great pair. You're kind and gentle and I've had enough of liaisons, I want to settle down and be naughty with one person for a long time. What do you say?'

My jaw drops. 'Charlie, are you serious? You must want something. What do you want?'

'No really, you're just my type and...'

I cut her off, 'No. Your type are males, tall, short, not so short not so tall. You crack me up.'

'I'm chatting you up here and you don't believe me.'

'I'm flattered, but I shall have to let you down.'

'You're so good with older woman, I thought maybe we ...?'

'Heavens love, you're only a month or two older than me and I feel like I'm entering my prime. Sorry to disappoint you.'

'Well it was worth. You should at least let me show you what you're missing.' A more determined salesperson I have never met. 'Well, what are you going to do when you're older eh?'

She always has a way of making me think.

'I want to be an outrageous bohemian artist.'

'Well boyo, a little practice wouldn't go amiss then. Would it?'

Belinda is oblivious to what's going on. Her head is stuck in the Venetian show. Bless her. But thankfully she's physically present in the gallery. I'm saved.

'How's it going, Belinda?' I call out to her.

She doesn't answer, and then I notice she's got small headphones in her ears. I walk over and, removing the headphones, ask again.

'Pink Floyd. It helps me think. *Wish You Were Here*. It's my favourite.' Well at least she has taste.

'Charlie's up to something. I can feel it in my bones.'

'Don't tell me she's after you again. She always says she'll get you one day.'

I don't know what to say. Apparently, there is one rule for the boss and a hundred that can be broken by the staff. Sometimes I think I'm the outsider here in this retail world. Maybe being an artist would be an easier life. Not so much guess work!

Charlie is full of smiles as she slinks up to me. 'Cup of tea?'

'What's the time?'

'Three o clock'

Wine o clock methinks. 'Glass of red then, please.' Memo to self, maybe I should drink a little less. 'A small one, not a flagon'

In truth I now know I have a problem with the permanently frisky member of my staff. I'm out of my depth. Best is to ignore it.

'I love Venice. It's such a romantic city. Isn't it?' Charlie's trying a different tactic.

'Well you can dream about it when the show's on and work your magic helping Belinda sell them to customers."

'That's the easy bit. Is Victor available?'

I smile thinking of Victor being attacked by Charlie. *Phew, I'm reprieved; it's over to you Victor. She's all yours dear friend.* Now there's a thought.

'What's so funny?'

Nothing at all.' I feel much better.

'I think the paintings are too cheap. They're magnificent and should be loads more expensive,' suggests Belinda.

'Well put that to Victor and let's see what he says. I must say I agree with you.' She is completely right and rising to the challenge.

'Really, that's so cool, thank you.'.

She rings Victor, who agrees without hesitation and we more or less double the prices. Here's hoping they sell anyway.

Another phone call, this time from the framer. All the works are ready to collect but for one slight problem; the framer himself has broken his ankle, slipping on his stairs at home and can't drive. *Can we collect them?*

A tall slender, well-groomed girl walks up to the desk as I'm hanging up. 'Hello, I'm Abi, Victor's niece.'

'Ah yes, we've been expecting a call from you. Your uncle said you might like to some work experience in a gallery.'

'I forgot to ring but I did have a look at your website and I can start as soon whenever you want. It's okay isn't it?'

'How can one refuse? Right, first things first. Come with me. We're off to collect your uncle's work'. We hail a taxi and Abigail's work experience formally begins.

Twenty minutes later at the workshop, I ask the driver to wait as outside his cab and we pass through the battered red door. We don't need to ring the old brass bell on the counter. Bill, the framer, is sitting there in a wheel chair looking stressed. 'Bloody stupid cat; went between my legs. Six weeks I've got to be in this ruddy cast.'

'Shall I sign it for you?' I won't repeat his expletives.

I introduce Abigail. 'This is Victors niece. You've just framed his show.' He sheepishly apologies for his outburst

Abigail nods 'I've heard worse. Mater dropped a vase on her foot once. It was rather expensive and it rolled onto the tiled floor and shattered. Her language was far worse; trust me.'

I like this girl. Her initial air of innocence, camouflages the woman in waiting.

All the paintings are bubble wrapped and thankfully numbered, making it easier to identify when hanging and labelling, but then dear reader, you know this already, don't you? It's a tight squeeze getting them all and the two of us into the taxi, but we manage it. Abigail's a natural packer. Experience Lesson One completed. Score 10 /10.

Lesson two is about unpacking, unwrapping and arranging paintings in an orderly fashion, without losing sight of the allocated numbering.

The static from the bubble wrap plays havoc with Abigail's long hair, which is flying away and standing on end. Belinda comes to the rescue with a can of something or other. I think it's called bonding. The display of friendship not the hairspray.

Belinda asks to be allowed to hang the show and I let her do it with Abigail's help. I find it amusing and rewarding to see how well I've developed her hanging skills and her managerial talents. It's not all plain sailing though. Belinda is on the fourth rung of the ladder when she utters a cry. 'Help, my finger's trapped in the cord!' Somehow the picture cord and the hook have attached themselves to her middle finger.

'Permission to touch? Do excuse me.' I lift her by her waist off the ladder, still connected to the painting. I return her to the floor; aware now that she's somewhat heavier than I realised or that I'm older than I like to remember and don't want to damage my back. 'How on earth did you manage to tie yourself up?'

'How on earth did you manage to lift me down?'

'I surprise myself sometimes.' I untangle her slightly blue looking middle finger from the painting. Thankfully the painting's undamaged.

The show's hung by teatime. I angle the lights for maximum effect. Lighting is so important to bring out the best in a painting. Please remember this little tip as so many electricians put stupid picture lights at the wrong height and the light doesn't even reach the painting. Just a little moan and dig.

'Voila! I think we should all have a celebratory drink. How about a nice bottle of Italian Red?'

The paintings have an exquisite glow to them and you can almost hear the colours rustling with atmosphere trying to escape from behind the glass. I have a good feeling about this show. I feel it in my stomach. Normally before an opening I experience a tension and nervousness, like a growing knot deep down. This time a serenity is developing. I'm sure it won't last but for now its drink o clock time. 'Cheers ladies. The gallery looks great. Here's to all of us.'

With two days to go, we're ready ahead of schedule, and everything's running smoothly. Now all we will need is a happy, buying audience.

I'm sure I mentioned two of my artists in my last book; Peter and Patricia, a husband and wife team. Today they drop in for unexpected visit. They tend not to leave their respective studios much so it's a pleasant surprise to see them.

Patricia says, 'I thought you might like a pot of my gooseberry jam.' She delves into her enormous black leather bag and follows the package with some helpful advice. 'Be careful. It tastes as sharp as a kitchen knife.'

'How lovely to see you both and how did you know Gooseberry's my all-time favourite jam?'

'I didn't, ducky. Pot luck one could say.'

Peter walks among the paintings 'I really like these. Very different from what you normally show. A touch of real class with a hint of innocence.' Peter's examination is slow and meticulous. 'Ah! He has a great palate too.' In the trade we call this intense scrutiny by the term *scanning*, and it's often conducted by rival artists before ever introducing themselves to mere mortal gallery owners.

'Drinks my dears?'

'Cup of tea would be lovely,' answers Patricia.

Belinda slips away to put the kettle on.

Charlie introduces Abigail. 'This is the artist's niece and she's been a great help the last couple of days. And these...,' she turns to Abigail, '...are my favourite artists!'

I cringe inside but Abigail's too smart for Charlie's mischief. She's already done her homework in my stockroom. 'What a pleasure to meet you, Peter. Variety is such an asset and I have to agree with Charlie. I'm struck by the boldness in your oils and the unusual use of greens and Patricia – your hand sewn pieces, - I'll own one, one day. I'm too used to Uncle Victor's paintings.

We grew up with his work everywhere round the house.'

Peter smiles, clearly enjoying the banter but Charlie's nose is, for some reason is put out of joint. *Game set and match to Abi.*

Patricia says, 'I think we should have one of these, sweetie. I love the light bouncing off the water.' Now this is a real compliment. An artist buying another artist's work in the same gallery they themselves show in. Very reassuring indeed. The magical red dot is placed on the said painting. Sold.

'Assume you want it left for the show. We can't make tomorrow evening.'

'Thanks, I'll drop it out to you afterwards and let you know how I get on with the jam.'

'How's your own painting coming on? Bet you never get any time mind you. I always say that a few minutes a day sketching is the best way forward.'

'I'll bear that in mind when I get a moment.'

Charlie says, under her breath 'Yes a moments fun would be a great idea. As for sketching, that's something else!'

Finally, it's Thursday and Victor plans to arrive early so we can chat about things What we certainly can't afford is to have a liquid lunch today. He's already late when the phone rings ominously. 'Hello ol' boy, spot of bother I'm afraid. The cars a bit broken. I'll leave it and taxi up to you.'

I knew it was going too smoothly. 'Are you okay?'

'I'm alright. Car isn't.' The phone goes dead. *Well at least he is still alive, so I can't put prices up just yet!*

'You look like you've seen a ghost,' says Belinda.

'Just a hiccup, I hope. Artists car demise, artist still alive.' *Can*

*anything else happen, a world war or an earthquake or something
less trivial perhaps?*

Abigail is less calm when she learns of Victor's delay. 'What's
happened? Is he alright?' I'm sure he shouldn't drive. He's
positively the worst person to sit behind a steering wheel.'

Having driven with him myself, I agree with her but it won't help
to say so. 'He assures me he's fine and will be here soon. We
have a couple of hours to go so let's all chill and break all the
rules and have a drink. Any one for a nice cup of tea?'

That inspires general laughter and Belinda emerges with a cold
bottle of fizz *and why not?* Victor arrives to find all of us
clutching half-empty, fluted glasses, and Charlie immediately
places a drink in his hand. 'You just might need this.'

'Oh, thank you. Hello Abi dear. How's Mama?' It's to be business
as usual; the car incident forgotten and on with the show.

Victor seems delighted with his exhibition and even more so
once he spots that there's already a sprinkling of little red dots
to be seen. 'It's rather splendid don't you think. I took the liberty
of asking a few more friends to pop along who already have
some of my work. Ah! Here they are now.'

He means the vintage couple straight out of a 1950s movie.
She; magnificent fur coat. He; double breasted, pin-striped suit.
Vintage; in their seventies but well preserved. They start to
chatter with Victor as soon as they're in the door. Let the show
begin.

Within minutes the place is a hive of loud conversation with
Victor greeting everyone and introducing guests to each other.
Wine is flowing, fizz is bubbling and even a peppermint tea is
produced on demand.

Soon to my satisfaction red dots are flying. Belinda grabs me by

the arm. 'They're all gone, every painting's gone. It's sold-out.'.
At that precise moment a voice I know only too well says, 'Hello darling, who is that young thing on your arm?' It's Penelope and she's not wearing her wedding ring.

'Welcome to my gallery. How lovely to see you. This is my senior sales executive, Belinda.'

Belinda says hello and vanishes into the crowd. What is it with female ESP? I'll never know.

Victor's in his element and taps a spoon against his glass. 'I'm delighted you could all make it today. Venice is such a magical place and there's so much going on throughout the day.'

'And night' someone calls out from the crowd. There's a titter of approval and Victor actually blushes.

'Well now, I've just been told that my show is a sell-out Thank you to the gallery for doing such a splendid job of hosting and hanging the show. I believe my niece has been involved in the process too. Well done Abigail dear, I won't embarrass you any further Thank you dear friends for all your support, wine and port over the years and for coming from far and near. There's only one more thing to say and that's cheers.' He gets the explosion of applause he thoroughly deserves.

'We shall have to celebrate afterwards,' Penelope says. 'I'm going to mingle, darling.'

It's hard to say how I feel at this moment, a mixture of happiness, delight, confusion, and relief. All accompanied by a touch of mischievous anticipation for what may happen later on.

I reckon this sums up being a gallery owner. You just never know what's going to happen next.

OLD RED LEATHER

Imagine a junkyard filled with enough *stuff* to fill three stage sets for *Steptoe and Son*. Add a few dogs, sheep and hunks of stone and you more or less have the place I'm visiting. However, there's one small difference. This place precariously overhangs a canal and looks like it's going to fall in at any moment. I proceed carefully. Very carefully.

The old green door with massive rusty hinges carries a sign. *Knock very hard*. I do exactly as requested and wait.

The more I look around, the more I spy. It's a very interesting zone; a throwaway museum of artefacts, strewn about randomly in a totally non-artistic way, waiting nervously to be adapted or utilised to make something. What that could be, I've no idea.

The door opens to reveal a completely dust covered chap in overalls and old hobnail boots. 'Greetings. Mind the flooring; it's a bit dodgy in places.'

Standing amongst breezeblocks, lathes and a colourful abstract in process mounted on an easel is an old-fashioned, chrome and red leather barber's chair. In addition, there are mirrors leaning up against wooden poles and crates. In all my years of visiting studios, I've never seen this sort of set up before. I have to ask. 'Work in progress. Installation perhaps?'

'No mate.' He laughs. 'I cut people's hair occasionally. Some of the women love it. Me names Rudolf but everyone calls me Randy'. A white dust covered hand is projected in my direction. I shake it carefully, trying to avoid a Saharan-scale sandstorm. Luckily, I'm not wearing any black clothing. Eureka, I've learnt from past experience!

The dust still flies everywhere, including up my nostrils and inevitably clogs the back of my throat. Trying to cough and still sound like a professional gallery owner, I attempt to strike up a relevant, fact-finding conversation. 'So what *cough* do you *cough, splutter* like to *cough, cough, gasp*, like the most in your art.' I stagger and reel into the barber chair.

'Well,' Randy says. 'All of it. Do you fancy a haircut?'

'No thanks. I like my hair as it is'

'Well, there's something about stone that really gets me going. Mind you I love to paint. But I get bored. Sculpting is what I really like...and the female form.'

His eyes are deep blue in his powdered face. You can see that there's a rough edge, an uncut diamond feel, about him.

'Don't you think you should wear a mask?'

'I should, but it stops me thinking!'

He roots around for a couple of mugs and pours nearly boiling water from a battered and dust covered kettle. 'Tea or coffee?'

'Weak tea please, no milk. No sugar.'

'Blimey. That's gnats piss. That ain't tea!'

We chat and I find him hugely likeable. He's refreshing and most certainly different. Mind you, I have to add that my gut instinct is saying *Lock up your daughters*, especially after he begins telling me some of the tricks he's got up to on his chair. All in the good name of art - I don't think!

Everything, the banter, the probing questions and answers, is all a means to an end though. It's a game or warfare; getting to know your opponents' cards even if you're not in a smoked filled room full of poker players. Money is the crux of it all. Will this sell? Will that work? Will you try to sell it for me? How much do you make? How much can I make? Will you try some back at your gaff? It's all the same, no matter who you're dealing with; a guessing game to get it right. Right for the customers and right for the artists and of course right for me who has to make a few bob if only to cover my time and all the overheads.

He feigns disinterest in money and he's not alone coz nobody wants to under-sell himself or herself and I've got to guess it just right. It's a highflying, juggling act, aided and abetted by careful assistants back my gaff. I like that word. *Gaff.* All my attempts to create a great successful art gallery, admired by many, reduced to a simple word. *Gaff.* Love it. It takes all the seriousness and all the goings on behind the scenes and throws them up in the air. I own a gaff. Isn't that just bloody perfect?

'Yes,' I say. 'I will take some pieces back to my gaff...if you clean them and remove all the dust.'

Randy looks at the stonework on the floor. 'A quick polish'll do the trick and I'll wrap them in blankets so you dain't ruin yer motor.'

His accent is pure Black Country, in case you haven't guessed. It's a refreshingly rare, old delight. I can't wait to invite him in to meet some of his future clients and collectors.

'Can I take a photo of you in your studio? It's for my new website so people can see what you're like and get a sense of the atmosphere surrounding your art'.

'Yeah. Why not?' He poses as only a natural could do.

My mind's racing ahead. I wonder if Charlie will try her luck with this one? Methinks there won't be any resistance from him. We shall have to wait and see. After a while, my car is laden with more than I care to think about. I'm sure the shock absorbers are none too delighted with half a quarry in the boot. However, the journey back's uneventful as the weight irons out any bumps and potholes in the road. Bless our country. The roads are crumbling. Long live the British Empire. Time for a radio four play for today!

Driving's the only head space I get. I enjoy listening to the airwaves. It's where I get to use my imagination whilst calming down and relaxing. Shame it's so rare that I get to hear the whole play and I never ever get to enjoy the whole of a five-part drama. Got no time. One day I suppose might. Something to dream about.

I arrive back at the gaff and enlist the help of my trusted team. 'Ladies, we have a new bod joining the stable. Help me bring these in please. Wait till you see the photos!'

After the pieces are strewn round the gallery, we play the *how much do you think we can sell them for* game.

Surprisingly it's Belinda who comments on the photo. 'Cor. He's a bit of alright then.' Think she approves. Charlie just seems bemused and if I could mind-read, I wonder if I'd find her thinking about a potential threesome.

Saturday morning arrives and in he walks, a stickily-built chap sporting a denim jacket, turned up jeans, heavy polished boots and a bobble hat. He has noticeably large bushy sideburns. Engelbert Humperdinck would be proud of those. He resembles nothing so much as a Liverpool docker. He slowly turns 360 degrees with his hands on his hips before giving his opinion. 'Nice gaff, chief.'

'Fancy a cuppa. No gnats piss, honest!'

'Smashing.'

'Ladies, let me introduce Randolph.'

'Everyone calls me Randy.'

Charlie's ears pick up and I swear I hear her mutter, 'I bet he is.' She turns to me and delivers that knowing smile of hers.

Belinda looks equally smitten - like she's about to donate her knickers and throw them at him. For a moment the gallery seems to have become a stud farm where willing cows wait in turn to be mounted by the bull. Everyone knows this, and my role is only to play at farm hand. What joy.

'You can play games after work, thank you. Belinda, show Randolph his inventory. I said *inventory*! And get him to sign the paperwork.'

'With pleasure,' she drools. They sit down in the far corner emitting chuckles and giggles at regular intervals. I've never seen Belinda acting so girly and coy. It's hilarious.

I stroll over with his cuppa. 'Here you are then; one cup of builder's brew.'

'Maybe Randy would like something stronger,' Belinda says, lovingly lost in our sculptor's eyes.

'I don't drink luv. Ta anyway. Tea's me favourite tipple. I used to drink like a horse and get into way too much trouble. I just about manage now with tea. Lots o' cups mind.' You would swear Adonis was talking with bells and angels flying around.

Belinda is seriously mesmerised and loses his attention only because a couple walk in to browse and the woman starts admiring one of Randy's pieces. In a jiffy he ups and introduces himself as the artist. Within five minutes she asks to buy the piece. Now that's amazing. It's a sort of sexual magnetism that does it, I think.

Belinda glides over to escort them to the desk to do the paperwork. That's an expression in the trade meaning *to pay*.

'It's alright this place. And your brew's good too.'

'Well, thank you. Hopefully we should continue to thrive a few more years now we have your seal of approval.'

Randy winks. 'Let me know if I can help out at any time. I forgot how much I enjoy selling. Easy innit when you know how.'

'Alright. I'll take a flyer. Let's do a meet the artist day with you. Turn up in your work clobber, but not as dusty please. Let's say two weeks Sunday. That's the 17th.'

'All right chief. Done. Ta very much.'

WISHY WASHY BLUE

Have you ever looked at a woman's hand and found it difficult to count the number of diamonds on her fingers? No? Well let me tell you!

This is a woman in her fifties in a full-length fur coat. 'Good morning. Are you the owner of this establishment?'

'I am indeed. A very good morning to you.' It seems like the right way to respond to her formality.

She glides over to the desk and sits down. Her seamed stockings flirt as her coat and dress fall away and she crosses and uncrosses her legs. A mighty fine pair of pins they are too. Very distracting.

'I have a problem and need some advice.'

'May I offer you a drink, fresh coffee or a fruit tea perhaps?' Why am I talking in this manner? Because she started it.

'My uncle has left me a folder of paintings and I have no idea what to do with them.'

'May I take a look?'

She opens her large leather bag; I can see the Mulberry emblem by the handle. From it she produces a red-ribboned folder and places it on the desktop. 'Here you are. Tell me what you think?'

I open the folder carefully exposing several tissue-covered watercolours. To my surprise they're all by a well-known deceased artist. 'Do you know who these are by?' I ask.

'No idea. I collect jewellery.' As if I hadn't noticed. *How does she keep her wrist so straight?* 'I simply have no inclination to put artwork on the walls. They ruin the wall paper.'

Good grief. I've heard many reasons for not hanging a painting before but this gets first prize.

'Well Miss... I'm afraid I don't recall your name...'

'I haven't told you yet. It's Maeve Denninger and it's Mrs.'

I do love being put in my place especially in my own gallery. Smile and start again. Opening the tissue carefully I expose a painting worth in excess of twenty-five thousand pounds. Well, the last one fetched that much at auction and here there are twelve of them, all at least as good. Not my style though and certainly not what I'd sell in the gallery. 'This artist has been well published over the last sixty years and it looks like some of these are originals and they've never seen daylight.' I'm intrigued

'My uncle told me he purchased them direct from the artist and then forgot all about them. They sat collecting dust on the top of his wardrobe. He offered them to me as a present two weeks ago and sadly he dropped down dead last week of a massive heart attack.'

'Do you actually own these then?' My eyebrows are raised,

waiting for the answer.

'Technically yes, but the funeral is next week and then the will has to be read.'

It's beginning to sound a bit too good to be true. My radar's spinning and lights are flashing in my head. Gut feeling, natural instincts, call it what you will. It's pushing me to believe these are stolen. Fortunately, there's an amazing website that one can use to check if works of art have been nicked.

'Let's check some prices for you.' I walk over the computer and type in the code to bring up the private site. Yes, the first is certainly stolen. There's an image of the print with the word *stolen* emblazoned in red across it and the rest of the paintings in the folder are mentioned too. Taken from the publishers no less.

I look up facing a pointed gun levelled at my nose. Take a deep breath. 'I don't believe you need to shoot me today...or any day.'

'You will do as you're told.'

'You have my undivided attention.' *Where are my staff when I need them?* I'm alone with a well-dressed, gun-wielding female thief. And a maniac to boot. I think this is where a TV commercial break would be most welcome.

I repeat 'Why would you want to shoot me?'

'Coz you're a man in a man's world and you bastards treat us female artists as secondary citizens and inferior to you bastard men."

'Okay I get it but you do hold a gun to my heard giving a distinct advantage to this situation.'

I try to smile and diffuse this dangerous situation. My insides reverberate, screaming with the thought that I'm going to die.

'Question. Do you think I should represent your art in this gallery?'

She stands up, walking around with the gun aimlessly pointed at the ceiling. She turns and spits out "How the fuck should I know? You know everything and you've refused to answer my requests.'

'Listen, I'm really sorry you feel this way but my approach is simple. Make an appointment and I see you at a mutually convenient time.'

'Fuck that! Now's the time and I want to be here in your gallery I am the best artist you will ever know.'

Seriously she's the most deranged artist that ever walked through my door. And I mean ever.

'I think we're getting off on the wrong foot here,' she says, tossing back hair.' I really am an amazing artist and I can be ever so nice and obliging.'

'Well I'd be most obliged if you stopped wielding and pointing that gun of yours.'

'Ha! Fooled you. It has the safety catch on. Watch.' She squeezes the trigger. There's an enormous bang and part of the ceiling comes down with dust everywhere. My ears are ringing and my heart is actually beating outside my body.

'What the FUCK. Isn't life fun? It's the same with sex don't you think. Fast loud and dangerous.'

'No, I don't.'

To my considerable relief the sound of the shot attracts the attentions of a passing police patrol. Two officers no less, pushing open the door. 'Is everything all right, Sir?'

'Oh, we're just having some fun, aren't we darling?'

Can't they see from my pleading expression that I'm at the mercy of a madwoman here?

'We heard a noise that sounded like gunfire coming from in here.'

'Not at all, officers. Darling, put the kettle on for these fine gentlemen, won't you?'

I'm totally not in control of my own life. *Help!!* One officer appears to have an *I don't believe you look* on his face so I mouth a warning at him. 'She has gun. Help. She's mad!'

'I didn't quite catch that, Sir.'

'Would you like tea or coffee?' I speak deliberately slowly and nod in a negating way.

'Are you all right, Sir? Something wrong with your neck?'

Maeve is holding the gun out again 'He's fine you bastard.' She aims it at the second police officer.

He says calmly to his colleague 'It was gunfire we heard. See, I told you so.' He slowly crosses to Mrs Denninger and in an act of casual bravery, pushes her with his flattened hand hard enough to knock her over. She falls against a glass bowl, sending it flying across the room. It shatters into far too many pieces to count and she drops the pistol as she goes down.

He picks up the gun with a handkerchief and sniffs the barrel. 'Freshly smoking I'd say.'

'Is it yours, Sir? A lovers' tiff. Are we being a naughty boy? Are you okay, Miss?'

'I'm fine,' she says. 'But he won't let me exhibit here and he's vile and vicious and I want him arrested officer.'

I can't believe this is happening at all.

'No' I shout back. 'She walked into my gallery and all hell's broken loose. She's mad. She has just tried to shoot me.'

Belinda appears from nowhere. About bloody time! 'I heard a noise, boss. Is everything all right?'

'Who's she? says Maeve 'I've not met her before. Is she your little bit on the side then, you bastard? How could you do this to me?' She spins round and sets off for the entrance.

'Not so fast, Miss' First officer is beginning to put his cogs into gear. I think we hear some whirling going on. 'Do you work here sir?'

'Yes, I do.'

'Do you work here ma'am?' The officer means Belinda.

'Yes!'

'Do you work here madam? He points at Maeve.'

She shouts back. 'I just want to exhibit my paintings. I'm an amazing artist and they won't show my work. Arrest them officers. NOW!'

The penny drops. Second officer grabs her arm. Fairly gently. 'Would you like to come with us my dear and we can file a complaint. Let's go together.' He walks Maeve Denninger out of the gallery and miraculously into a waiting police car, parked outside.

'It looks like she's on the loose again. Such a shame. Some people should be locked up, not medicated in my opinion.

Did I hear correctly? My ears were still ringing from the gunshot. I think I've just been presumed innocent till proven guilty.

The officer continues unfazed. 'May I take a few details? Is this your gun?'

'No officer. It's her's. I only met it for the first time today whilst it was attached to that woman. Which hospital has she escaped from?'

'They don't escape you know. It's care in the community. After all, they do have rights you know!' He turns, flips his small black notebook closed and walks out the gallery without a by your leave or even handing over the usual business card in case I remember anything else. There's only one word that springs to mind and I'm too polite to use it.

Belinda collects up a bundle of papers from the floor and presents them to me. 'What shall we do with these wishy-washy watercolours?'

'I'm not doing anything. They're in your hand and I say *well volunteered*. They're all yours! Every fucking last piece of wishy-washy paper! I need a bloody large drink! Or a holiday! You deal with them! Bloody hell! Nearly shot dead in my own gallery!'

'Oh dear! Are we having a bad day then?' says Charlie bringing forth a large rioja.' Her entry is perfectly timed, unlike being shot in the ceiling. Which isn't a tax-deductible expense.

Today is not a perfect day, whatever Mr. Lou Reed might have to sing on the subject.

STRONG GREEN

In all the years I've worked my gallery, I've only occasionally been asked to give a talk but today's one of the days. A group of business people called the CRBL gather quarterly as an excuse for a glorious piss up, consuming vast quantities of beer and wine, usually both and claim It all back on expenses. How nice! After all this time, my accountant still doesn't accept that wine is an integral tool for selling in art galleries. And it has to be good wine too - none of your three for a tenner stuff!

Anyway, I have to be booted and suited like a sheep to fit in. Well sod that! I'm sporting tweed trousers with a shocking purple stripe, a bright orange spotted shirt and no tie, and a vintage leather jacket with two badges on it, one saying *What's the use of getting sober* and the other *When you gonna get drunk again?* The latter refers to a brilliant Louis Jordan song covered by Joe Jackson on his *Jumpin' Jive* album — see I'm a mine of useless information!

Herein lies the lesson; orange and purple are complementary colours, so they harmonise. How I wear them possibly might not but who cares? Not I. I hover around the gallery somewhat nervously. For what reason I cannot fathom, Belinda pays me a compliment. 'You look really cool for a change.'

'For a change?'

My head is whirling even though I do have a good idea what to say. I've even made a few notes but you have to be careful and read the audience properly. Anyway, enough of pacing the gallery floor. Here I go.

'Have fun' Belinda waves with a mock smile, as if sending me off to the slaughter house.

My taxi arrives and we drive across town to the Cornwall Hotel. It has a smart Georgian facade with two huge columns and vast oak doors. A large doorman, dressed in morning suit and top hat, opens the taxi door and the look on his face is a priceless. He obviously recognises a well-dressed gent when he sees one.

It's showtime. I proffer no tip and walk deliberately through into the heady atmosphere of a mausoleum. The place is exceptionally quiet. It has that padded cell quality. Not that I've ever been in a padded cell. The carpet is a rich green wool, several inches deep and carries a monogram in the form of a letter C in a shield, emblazoned at ten intervals. Not that I notice petty details like that you understand!

Following a CRBL sign and an arrow takes me to the Admiral Suite, along a corridor with a collection of old nautical paintings and prints hanging on both sides. The suite is the furthest room from the reception and the door is closed. Such a friendly warm place. Reminds me of a graveyard I visited in Rome back in the eighties. I open the door to be greeted by roomful of women in business suits. Some wear smart pencil skirts but most seem to be in trouser suits. There are two butlers with mortician's faces pouring teas and coffees from silver polished pots into delicate bone china tea-cups. There's not a wine glass in sight. To be daring, they're offering a selection of apple, cranberry and orange juices as an alternative. What a refreshing change! In fact, quite novel. I think this is going to be quite interesting. Possibly.

A well-set blonde hairdo casually strolls up to me. 'You must be the gallery chap. We are looking forward to your talk. Which museum are you from again?'

'Actually, I'm not from any museum, I have my own gallery which promotes living artists.'

She looks stunned. 'Shula said you were a curator in her notes. She sends her apologies for not being here this afternoon. Are you sure you're not from a museum?'

'Quite. I left my establishment an hour ago and as far as I remember, it was still selling contemporary art.'

'Stay here a moment. I'll get Sharon. She'll know what's what.'

You know that feeling when you've entered the room for a

function and after shaking a few hands the penny drops and you realize you're in the wrong place, with the wrong wedding party or even at the wrong funeral.

Sharon hastily appears, 'There seems to be a misunderstanding. We were expecting a talk on how to curate an exhibition.'

'Ah well that's more or less what I do.' I mentally rip up my notes on how to run an art gallery. 'I curate exhibitions with the aim of selling all the works. It saves storing them afterwards.'

'Really!' Sharon sounds more interested now.

'Really!' I nod. I'm not sure I'm out of the shit yet but it sounds good. 'I've curated exhibitions as far away as Edinburgh you know.'

'Follow me.'

I do as I'm told. We walk to the head table and take our seats. I'm sitting with Sharon on my left, a lady called Phyllis to my right and along from her a woman who looks just like Margaret Rutherford in a black business suit. I know that's not an easy image to conjure up but give it a go.

Lunch is served. Cauliflower soup followed by quiche and salad. I hate quiche; it's a pointless scrambled egg mush in a pastry.

Margaret Rutherford stands to go through the formalities and then hands the room over to me. Well there's only one thing for it. Sink or swim and believe me, I've learnt to swim.

'Ladies, what a privilege it is to stand here in front of the best-dressed lunch group I've ever attended in all my years in the art world.' There's a silence in the room so I continue 'Far too often one has to do breakfast meetings at some ridiculous o'clock, lunch-time previews and openings and all too often these are noisy, badly dressed events. I know I shouldn't say this, but in the art world you tend to notice these things. They're attended by people, mostly men, who bore the pants off me. I make no apology for not wearing a tie, I couldn't find one to complement this shirt.' Suddenly there's applause followed by a ripple of laughter. Bloody hell, I've nailed it!

The rest becomes easier with the talk changing direction. I throw in a few anecdotes on how to hang paintings in the right way, a few anecdotal tales of art, artists and clients; it's apparent that a little gossip goes a long way, no matter how well one is dressed.

Question time, and a very smartly fitted suit stands up to ask about my policy on female artists. I say, 'Madame, I would never take on a female artist. They're far too dangerous for the likes of mere mortal men.'

She smiles and you guessed it; 'My mother is an artist. How can I get her into your gallery?'

'Through the front door, and a drink will be on hand if she likes. We offer a fine selection of teas, coffees and wines. It's my humble opinion that wine oils the wheels of the art world.'

Then it's done. 'Would you like a drink young man? We have a policy to refrain till after the speaker has finished. Sometimes you need one then you know?'

'That's a lovely idea. Thank you.' Need one? Try three!

I'm presented with a bottle of port and thanked by Phyllis. Everyone stands to give a round of applause and a bar miraculously opens up at the rear of the room. I swear it wasn't there before. I'm saved. I've lived to tell the tale.

I walk into the gallery and Charlie is busying herself with a young chap. She turns and sniffs at me. 'You smell of perfume!'

'Good afternoon to you too. I've been in a hotel suite with a whole lot of well-dressed ladies of business.'

'I bet you have,' and she continues to woo her unsuspecting client into something rather special for his bedroom wall.

CRIMSON RED – THE FINAL CURTAIN

A letter arrives in a brown envelope with an unusual postage stamp. It's splattered in some foreign language I don't recognise. Belinda opens it in her usual debonair manner and stares at the contents awhile. 'I don't think you're going to like this one bit.' She hands the letter to me and heads for the kitchen. 'I'll get you a drink.'

> *Dear Sirs.*
>
> *We act on behalf of clients who have purchased the building you occupy who intend to redevelop the block.*
>
> *Accordingly, we are serving notice under BLAH BLAH BLAH to vacate the premises by the 3rd November this year.*
>
> *If any problems arise from compliance with this correspondence please put them in writing to our office for due consideration.*
>
> *Yours sincerely*
>
> *Mr. Nonentity*

Shit shit shit! They can't do this surely? I've been here twenty years, give or take. I don't know how I feel. Numb? Frozen maybe. Surely, they cannot do this without more notice? Surely not? Or can they? A thought crosses my knitted brow. It's a sign. I could move...I could cry...I could....I should, I would.

There is only one thing to do.

I will party. The gallery will show its appreciation to all its artists and customers over the years. After all, if in doubt, there is only one thing to do and that's to party hard.

'Belinda. You can come out now'.

The door opens sheepishly to admit a red eyed assistant. Belinda's bottom lip quivers. 'Is this for real?' she mutters.

'Bloody well looks like it. I'll ring my solicitor and find out. This will cost. I can feel it in my bones and my bones' bank account won't like it one bit.'

A thought. The wine shop is going to have to close as well. So, we'll have to make this an even larger do than when we opened up. I must be mad. Although...here's an opportunity to do what I've always wanted. To paint.

Charlie arrives late in her usual, effervescent *I met a man last night self*-persona. 'I love a party. Who's the artist this time?'

Belinda begins to cry again. 'It's not an artist. It's the end. It's the death toll party. The gallery is being knocked down.'

'We can open another somewhere surely?' Charlie's voice rises a decibel or two 'No! They can't do this. I love working here. You must find somewhere else to open. Surely?' She looks me hard in the eye. 'Does this mean we can at least...'

'Don't even go there.'

'You're such a spoilsport sometimes.'

'Shall we advertise we're closing. A pre-obituary statement.' Belinda drops back into work mode.

'I don't think so. Let's Just invite some friends.' I too begin to well up inside. 'One last time eh!'

'Everyone knows you. Invite everyone.'

'Listen up my dear trusty team. Sometimes in life shit happens for a reason. You have to look at the positive and today's is in the fridge. Bring forth that large bottle of champagne. It's under the Chablis. Let's start the wake now.'

The pop of the cork may not change the atmosphere but the second glass of fizz starts to thaw the women.

'To my great team.'

Charlie gives me a large hug, squeezing too tight. She whispers in my ear. 'You really don't know what you're missing. Thank you for the fun. I'll let my little dream win.'

'Maybe in another life! Shall I come back as your gardener or your butler?'

The invite we decide to issue does not say we're closing down. We pick something more dramatic. *Le finale.*

However, today still has to be business as usual. One has to keep paying the bills.

The first old customer of the day through the doors is Mrs. Topping, with a young chap on her arm. She's wearing a long pleated, cream skirt with a matching, almost see-through, blouse. The smile on her face lights up like a heading on a Sunday paper. 'Ah champagne. What's the occasion?'

We all look at each other. Nobody's sure what to say.

'Love,' says Belinda. 'All you need is love!'

'Well, we'll drink to that, won't we Brad?'

The three of us smile knowingly at each other. *We know what you've been doing!*

'I'm looking for a little something as a thank you,' says Mrs.

Topping.

'Let's see what we've got hidden in our stockroom Mrs.T. Follow me.'

She lightly trips along in my wake and whispers in my ear. 'Isn't he a dish? I feel like I've come back to life. Mind you I'm still disappointed you haven't phoned me. You should have.'

I'm almost speechless. 'My loss.' I nod. Then to business. 'May I ask how much you'd like to spend on this thank you?'

'Just a couple of grand,' she says. 'He's better value than joining the gym.' She pokes me in the ribs with her elbow.

I show her a few things, unwrapping boxes and pulling out etchings. I don't believe she really cares what she buys. She's come in to display her new workout. How sweet. Memo time; never underestimate the power of a woman on a mission. Actually, change that. Never ever underestimate the power of a woman full stop.

This should put the bloody feminists to rights.

My accountant rings telling me to put all the paperwork in order and remind me that I have to keep every bit of it for six years for tax purposes. Oh, such joy.

It doesn't take long for the news to spread. Well there's no news like bad news and it does bring people in. The masses gather for the cull. Everyone wants a bargain. I suppose it's human nature to grab what you can. I decide to abstain from drinking till closing night. Don't ask me why. It's a protest of sorts or a self-depriving punishment for all the good times. To the outside world it's business as usual but inside I feel like this is the precursor to doing what I want to do. What have I got to lose? My sanity went out the window years ago. I must stop talking to myself.

The sad thing is there are still good artists wanting appointments to see me and I hate saying no. Some don't believe I'm refusing them and are quite rude. One chap actually wrote to say spent five years building up the confidence to ask. Maybe I should reply *Come back five years ago*. No that's not fair. Time travel doesn't exist. Apart from rushing forward towards foreclosure.

It all hits home when the landlords enter with two suited gents. Their trousers are too short so they must be officials. One has a clipboard and the other a memo tape recorder. He flicks the mike on and off annoyingly.

'How long has that pipework been on show?' says official number one. Is he talking to me?

I say nothing. The landlord repeats the same question.

'Before you gave me the lease, I believe. You should know!'

Official number two clicks his mike and mutters something.

'Is there any reason for you to just walk into my shop unannounced while my business is open. This is an invasion of my rights as a tenant and I request you leave now. Make an appointment, preferably after the end of November '

Over at my desk I pick up the phone and dial the local paper. 'Hello, is that the press office?'

The landlord says, 'Can I have a word?'

'Any particular reason?'

'There might be a problem with that pipe.'

'Well now you tell me! That's your problem matey, not mine. When you've ripped the whole building down I'm sure you'll resolve it.'

'We'll have to renegotiate your exit terms based on the pipework. It's not legal.'

'I give you ten seconds to remove yourself from these premises or that pipe of yours will be shoved right up your...' I stop myself from saying the word. I'm physically shaking. 'OUT!' I shout. 'NOW!' Even louder.

The three men leave. It feels like war's been declared.

'Blimey, I wouldn't want to get on the wrong side of you' says Charlie flicking her hair back. 'At least, not in the daytime.'

'Right, that's it. The biggest damned party ever. Bring it on. Ladies to war!'

It's impossible to guess how many will attend, which means it's impossible to cater correctly, so we decide not to have food, just massive bowls of sweets, biscuits, wine gums; all things stupidly silly and childish. There'll be live music too. Where the hell will they go? Who cares? Let's stuff the place to the ceiling and go out in style.

As the day draws nearer a knot grows in my stomach. Am I doing the right thing? Why not open somewhere else? Except that I've been there, I own the t shirt - printed and designed it myself. But what will Belinda and Charlie do when we close? Memo; give them glowing references and a farewell bonus.

And on the other hand; no more paperwork, no more VAT or insurance and all the myriads of stress just to function No more 24/7 active alarm systems. Peace, yes peace. No more customers, artists pain in the derrieres, and no more breakfast meetings. I'm going to be an artist, broke or not.

It's a sunny day, and I sit with Belinda and Charlie having a coffee before the expected mayhem breaks forth. Usually a pre-brief has involved a quick snifter across the road in the wine bar, but today we're espresso fuelled. 'There's only one thing I want to say to you two; sell everything, anything that moves, you name it; deal and deal again; take no prisoners. Let's go team.' We stand up to leave.

'Paying for the coffees, sir?' The waiter hands me the bill.

'Sorry, I'm a bit preoccupied 'I put a tenner in his hand. 'Keep the change.'

There's a massive bouquet of flowers leaning outside the door. The unsigned card says *Goodbye and good luck*. I haven't the foggiest idea who it's from. Belinda scoops them up, finds a vase and displays them right in the middle of the gallery.

People start to trickle in from about midday. It's a help yourself bar, coz for once we're going to all be hands on deck selling off everything. Slowly the gallery fills and the noise levels increase. You can't hear the music now for the noise of conversations getting louder and louder. There's a violin player trying to move around serenading anyone who wants to listen. Whose stupid idea is this? I take no responsibility this time. In passing he says to me in a lilting Irish brogue. 'I can't hear a feckin' thing. I'm not sure if me fiddle's even in tune.'

'I'm not sure I know why you're even here, if that helps!' He appears a tad upset and fiddles his way into a corner.

Artists mingling with customers isn't usually a recommended combination but it's the dying moments of my gallery and I don't care. You can all do whatever you like. And that's exactly what everybody's doing. Even I get the odd pinch on the bum. Really, you just can't trust the public these days.

Belinda grabs my arm and shouts in my ear, 'How much do you want for the desk?'

'What do you reckon? A ton!'

She laughs out loud 'That's exactly what I'm thinking.'

Lots of everything is selling. 'Will you throw in that vase if I buy these paintings'. *With pleasure madam, please pay over there.*

The music is blaring; people are actually dancing. If it stands still long enough it will sell. Charlie's on top form, Belinda's the cavalry and all the sweets are being devoured. Strangely we haven't run out of booze yet. My trusty chair is sold. The countless decisions made in it, good riddance. *Yes, I'm sure it will look lovely in your office, thank you.*

You'd like a piece of the gallery as a memento? 'Do you like pipework? I have a rather unusual bit for sale if you like. Oh, never mind. How about a glass cabinet with some superb glass to display?'

Belinda pulls my arm. 'Someone wants to buy the plan chest. Come into the stock room now.' I follow her, marching quickly. She slams the door, throws her arms around me and kisses me on the lips. 'You're wonderful. It's been the best job ever.'

I hold her close. 'Thank you. Do you want the plan chest? If so it's yours.'

'No, I've already sold it. I just had this urge to kiss you.' And she returns to the fray.

I'm humbled, with a genuine feeling of having achieved something. Before I owned my own gallery I'd never had a business of my own before and my assistant chief tells me it's been the best job ever. The kiss is the best bonus I could ever deserve.

Back in the main room, the world is going into fast forward and everything and everyone is a bit of a blur. My mind goes back to the opening, my naivety in opening the gallery *How the hell did I get myself into this?* I suddenly feel very sad. I should feel proud.

I hear the *Harry Lime* theme playing in the back of my mind; the zither striking my heartstrings. I shout out for everyone to be quiet and wait a few seconds. 'Friends, clients and artists, lend me your ears.'

I feel a tear rolling down my cheek. Not now! Don't cry. Come on, hold it together. 'This gallery wouldn't have been anything without you all. The symbiotic relationship between artists, customers and staff has, I always like to say, put colour into all our lives and I want to thank you all, especially my dream team who've put up with my little idiosyncrasies over the years. Looks like everything is selling and remember, everything has to go. Except me.'

'How much' shouts somebody in the crowd. There are massive cheers and the room is full of laughter. My back is being slapped as if I've just won a heavy-weight-boxing match. We party into the evening and beyond. The last guest, who I'm sure wasn't invited, leaves at three minutes to two in the morning. The gallery is no more.

'Well ladies, that's how you throw a closing down party.'

'Where shall we go now? 'Charlie asks

'Is she serious? says Belinda. 'I'm cream crackered'

'Home I believe is a good idea,' I say

'Can we come with? How about one last glass of something. Just the three of us?'

'Come on Belinda, the night is young and you're supposed to be young too. Trust your aunt!'

'Can't think of a reason why not.'

'Taxi!'

Next morning I'm standing outside the shop looking through

the plate glass window, staring at my past. It's all gone Everything's been collected and the place is empty. As vacant as the week before we opened, all those years ago. What will never go are the memories and friends and all the mayhem stored in my head. Still, I've given the keys back to the landlord without wishing him well. How remiss of me. And that's that.

The twenty years seem to have flown by in a moment. I feel emotional again before the sense of freedom reasserts itself, a release you could say despite my brain screaming out in total panic, *What the hell am I going to do now?*

The answer's on the road in front of me. A woman walks right up to me. She's wearing a sloppy, cream-coloured jumper, along with a great pair of legs, revealed by sprayed on drainpipe jeans capped off by a pair of very expensive, crimson patent-leather, stiletto, ankle boots. Not that I notice such details.

'Hello, stranger' she says in a familiar gravelly voice, I recognise immediately. It's Miss Top Hat and Tails.

How odd. The last time we met was when I'd hired her for the opening night of the gallery

'Hello. How are you? Where have you been? I've not seen you in years? What are you doing in this neck of the woods?'

'Hang on Whoa! So many questions. Not a lot. Been working away, you know the sort of thing. I've been thinking of looking in to see you for ages so I thought I'd see what you're up to. Have a spot of lunch or maybe something else. What's happened here? What you done with the gallery?'

'The gallery's closed forever. Had to get out. The landlord's redeveloping the block and I'm about to embark on the next phase of my life.'

'Oh yeah. What's that going to be then; a teacher, or let me guess, an art consultant. You know, something boring?'

'Not in the slightest. I'm going to do what I've always wanted to do since I was a teenager.' I take a gulp as if was about to confess that I've lost my virginity. 'I'm going to be an artist myself.'

'No kidding! Really. You! That's so funny. Fancy a muse?'

'I've never been more serious. I'm going to look after one artist, me, from now on. So, what are you doing the rest of your life?' My heart stops for a moment, thinking what I've just said.

'I fancy an adventure. Life should never be normal' she says.

'You might have to stick around forever though. That's the deal'

'Don't you mean committed?'

'I rest my case,' and offer her my arm. She puts hers through mine and we walk along the pavement to nowhere in particular. *Lunch with a muse. Now there's a start.*

She squeezes and looks up at me. 'Nice biceps. I like a man with good muscles. Oh yes, and a cute bum.'

Life is good.

The newly retired gallery owner will return in 2019...

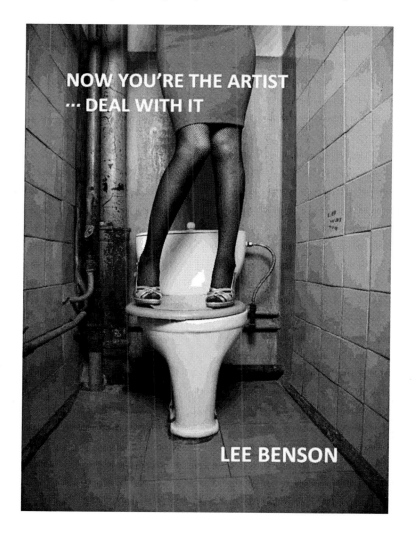

FICTION FROM APS BOOKS

(www.andrewsparke.com)

Lee Benson: *So You Want To Own An Art Gallery*

Lee Benson: *Where's Your Art gallery Now?*

Andrew Sparke: *Abuse Cocaine & Soft Furnishings*

Andrew Sparke: *Copper Trance & Motorways*

HR Beasley: *Nothing Left To Hide*

Jean Harvey: *Pandemic*

Michel Henri: *The Death Of The Duchess Of Grasmere*

Nargis Darby: *A Different Shade Of Love*

TF Byrne: *Damage Limitation*

Lee Benson is also the author of the Henry Egg children's stories which are also published by APS Books.